FIGHTING WORDS

Fighting Words is a creative writing centre established by Roddy Doyle and Sean Love. It opened in January 2009 and aims to help students of all ages to develop their writing skills and to explore their love of writing. It provides story-writing field trips for primary school groups, creative writing workshops for secondary school students, and seminars, workshops and tutoring for adults. All tutoring is free. See www.fightingwords.ie.

Coláiste Dhúlaigh Post Primary School is a co-educational school located in Coolock, Dublin 17. See www.colaistedhulaighpp.com.

FIGHTING WORDS

Stories by
Transition Year
Students from
Coláiste Dhúlaigh

FIGHTING WORDS
THE WRITE TO RIGHT

in association with

NEW ISLAND *Open Door*

FIGHTING WORDS
First published 2011
by New Island
2 Brookside
Dundrum Road
Dublin 14

www.newisland.ie

A CIP catalogue record for this book is available from the British Library

ISBN: 978-1-84840-101-3

New Island receives financial assistance from The Arts Council (An Chomhairle Ealaíon), Dublin, Ireland.

Typeset and cover design by Mariel Deegan
Printed by Drukarnia Skleniarz

10 9 8 7 6 5 4 3 2 1

Acknowledgements

Thanks to everyone at Fighting Words, in particular:

Joan Harman
Mimi Valiulis
Brian Herron
Melatu Okorie
Caitlin Lewis
Laura Cassidy
Oonagh O'Farrell
Orla Lehane
Sheila O'Flanagan
Patricia Scanlan

Thanks to the students at Coláiste Dhúlaigh, and to their teacher, Kathy Jones.

Contents

Introduction

There is a famous short film of the footballer, Diego Maradona. It was made when he was a child. He is doing tricks with a ball. It is brilliant and lovely and funny, because we know that the child became one of the best footballers ever.

Now, imagine reading the first story that Maeve Binchy ever wrote. Before we knew her name. Before we read her books. Before she even wrote her books. When she was still at school. It would be brilliant too, a little sneaky look at what was going to come.

This new book is bit like that. It is a collection of stories by writers who are just starting. They are still in school – Coláiste Dhúlaigh, in Coolock, in Dublin. They were 15 or 16 when they wrote the stories. Once a week, they went to a place called Fighting Words, near Croke Park, and wrote.

They wrote about love and friends. They wrote about the mistakes we make and the lessons we learn. They wrote about emigration. They wrote about vampires and football and fighting. They wrote about what Irish writers have been writing about for hundreds of years. But they wrote in a way that is fresh and exciting.

Emma Browne's story, 'Could This Be Love?', is about two people getting to know each other – the embarrassment, the fun, the things that go right and wrong. It has the best line about falling in love that I have read in years: 'We got curry chips.'

'Paula's Story' by Klaudia Bucka is full of great writing. 'School is horrible, everything is sad colours; no pink, no yellow, no orange, no red.' It also has 'them' – vampires.

'Help!' by Megan Burke is a dark, realistic story. Step by step, it describes a girl's fall, and rescue. The mistake is made, and the lesson is learnt.

Hughie Collins, the writer of 'Junior Night', is a born story-teller. This is his first sentence: 'I'll tell you a little story, so relax and enjoy.' I read it and thought, 'Oh, oh.' The ending is very funny. I didn't want to laugh – but I did.

'The Fight Life' by Gary Duffy is a tough, well-written story. The fight scenes are excellent. Gary Duffy writes about a hard, violent world. But it is also a love story.

Eve Gibney's story, 'The Perfect Ending … Or Is It?', is full of life and very funny. 'Brooke had bags up to her elbows, full of dresses and shoes.' Only someone who loves words could write a great sentence like that.

Sarah Gorry wrote 'Today, Tomorrow, Forever?' and she also loves words. 'Alex didn't like the word "babe". It reminded her of the movie about the pig.' Two short sentences, but we already know a lot about Alex – and about the writer.

'Fresh Start' by Shannon Granger is set in San Francisco, but one of the characters is 'a complete waster'. Dublin meets America. 'She had been blinded by love. Until that night, when he hit her.' These are frightening words, written by another born story-teller.

'In Love' by Danielle Hand is about loss and happiness. It also has the key to true love: 'They walked and talked. Sasha laughed at his jokes even though they weren't funny.'

Eoghan Higgins gives a great account of *that* match in Paris, in 'Le CHEAT'. But it has a happy ending. 'The French team came last in their group, the manager was fired and several players were suspended. Ireland's summer wasn't *all* bad.'

Alan Keegan's 'The Dressing Room' is a well-told story about friends drifting apart, and coming together again. 'Life was too short to hold a grudge.'

Damien McKevitt's 'Rotten Centre' is strange, for all the right reasons. It is mad, and full of great images, like 'breathing sand'. I wish I had written that one.

Tomás Nguyen's story, 'My Friends and Me', has great short, punchy sentences, and a great twist at the end. Then there's the way he uses the word, 'buzz' – 'a buzz', 'the buzz', 'buzz around', 'buzzing up'. It's like watching the invention of a new word.

Karen Nolan's 'Love Story' is exactly that, a love story. But it has a twist. It also has another great description of love: 'They were chatting so much that the bus drove past.'

'WHY?' by Megan Tyrrell is a wonderful story about that big question, 'Who am I?' It is full of little details that made me believe every word. Stacy, the main character, writes her phone number on a receipt. I could see her doing it.

One of the stories ends with the simple statement, 'Life is good'. After reading the stories by these new young Irish writers, I agree. Life *is* good.

Roddy Doyle,
2011

Could This Be Love?

Emma Browne

It came to 10.15 a.m. and our bus arrived. We were all going mad to get the back seats on the bus. We were going on an overnight trip to Slane.

John was saying to Robbie, 'If you don't save me a seat I'm going to throw you in the bog down here!'

While the rest were saying, 'Miss, can we go to Centra? We're starving.'

We had a great laugh on the bus. All of us had bonded as a transition year group, because we've known each other for a few years now.

The bus was very small, so I was put beside a boy named Luke. I was very shy and I didn't really talk to Luke. He was always very close to the boys.

My two friends, Shannon and Robbie, started whistling at Luke and saying, 'You two make a lovely couple.'

I was mortified, but Luke just sat there saying, 'Oh shut up, you two, and don't be so stupid. As if I would ever be with her.'

When the group first got to the farm, we were all like, 'OH MY GOD, this is stupid! We're not going out in that rain!'

The weather was horrible – it was lashing rain, and windy.

Catherine, who was showing us around the farm, was very nice and she bonded with all of us.

She brought us into a dark room and told us were going Irish dancing. We were all laughing and saying, 'Who do you think we are? We're not looking like those!'

Catherine explained to us what it was going to be like, and we all found it interesting. She split us up into groups to dance. I was put with Luke!

Again!

I wasn't happy because I thought he was a show off. He kept saying, 'I'm not dancing with her. Will ye put me beside someone else, Miss?'

He went to sit down a few times and was refusing to dance with me.

I was mortified for the second time that day. And here I was in the room, standing by myself. Embarrassed. Everybody had a partner except me.

But a few minutes later Luke got up in a huff and started dancing with me anyway.

It started off very slowly. Then it suddenly went all doo-wha-diddly-bob-bops, up and down, and up and down, spinning all over the room. We did not realise we were having such a good time.

I never saw myself ever having fun with Luke.

We finished Irish dancing and then we got on a tractor to take us to the bog. I told myself all day I wasn't going to jump in.

But then I decided to jump in after all. It looked like fun.

But then I got stuck.

I was laughing one minute and crying the next.

Luke was laughing! I could see that he cared about me being stuck, but he also cared what everyone else would think. Then he helped me out.

He sat beside me in the tractor on the way home to the house, and we got on well. But he acted so differently when he was with his friends and I didn't know why.

When we got back to the house we were staying in, I ran up to the room and had a shower.

I was very dirty from the bog. I was kind of thinking about why Luke acted so differently to me in front of all his friends.

My friend Shannon said to me: 'Emma, are you all right?'

I said, 'Yeah, I'm grand. I just don't get why Luke is so nice to me when he's on his own, and not nice when he with all his friends.'

'He acts like that when he secretly likes someone and doesn't want to admit it,' said Shannon.

After Shannon told me this, I kind of just forgot about it.

It came to nine o'clock that night and we were all sitting up in the games room having a laugh. Luke and I were not really taking any notice of each other. We were being cool.

The owners of the place we were staying at made us a little snack before we had to go to our rooms.

We were all sitting at the table, and Luke started talking to me because his friends weren't around. But when they came in, he ignored me!

This made me very angry and upset.

****

It was late at night and I woke up needing to go the toilet. I was walking down the stairs and I saw Luke sneaking out for a smoke. I tried to ignore him because I didn't want to talk to him, but then he called me.

'What do you want?' I said.

'Can I talk to ye for a sec? Please?'

'Yeah, make it quick though.'

So he sat me down and explained to me that he didn't mean to be so ignorant that day. He was being very friendly and nice to me. Then he started saying:

'Megan, I actually realised I fancied you today, and I didn't know what way to act with you. So I guess that's why I was ignoring you when the boys came in, because I didn't want to tell them.'

When he told me this I got butterflies in my stomach, because I did have a tiny crush on Luke beforehand, but never told anyone.

I felt very happy about what Luke had said to me. We sat talking for ages, but it was getting very late.

'Luke, as much as I would love to sit here all night and talk to ye, I have to go up to my room. I only came down for a wee.'

'Ah, it's grand; we can talk again, I hope.'

I got very excited. But I just smiled at him and said, 'Goodnight, Luke.'

I was chuffed with the talk we'd had.

I felt great.

****

The next morning I felt a bit nervous going downstairs. I was wondering if Luke was going to say anything to me.

He was there at the bottom of the stairs, standing with his friends.

'What's up, Megan? You all right?'

'Hiya, Luke; yeah, I'm grand.'

'OK, I'll talk to you on the bus.'

I was so happy. I told my friends what Luke said to me the night before and they were all happy for me, saying, 'Wooo, Megan! Get stuck in there!'

We were walking out of the house going to get on the bus, and I heard Luke saying, 'Boys, I'm going to sit beside Megan, OK?'

So I sat at the window.

I was very nervous, hoping Luke would sit beside me. But then, when he finally came and sat next to me, I wasn't nervous at all. I was real happy.

Both of us were having a great conversation and I could tell he was dropping hints to have my number. So I gave him my number; he looked happy.

He said to me, 'I'm going to ring you so you'll have my number.'

I just started laughing. 'Yeah, OK.'

****

The bus took us to Fantasia to play bowling.

When we got there we were discussing the teams, and Luke said to me, 'Megan, do ye want to go for something to eat?'

So I said, 'Yeah.'

We got curry chips.

'So what's going to happen now? Are we going to see each other when we're home from the trip?' asked Luke.

'I don't mind, Luke; it's up to you,' I said.

He said he would love to. I was delighted.

We finished our food and went to play bowling. We had a laugh, and later got on the bus to drive home. We all had a great laugh on the bus. We had a big sing-song.

****

When we were home, Luke and I kept in contact by phone, because he lived in Malahide and I lived in Coolock. I told my ma and da about us on the trip. They were happy for me.

The next day, Luke and me met up and went to the cinema and we had a great day out.

****

Two weeks on, Luke and me were still seeing each other and were enjoying each other's company.

Then it was a month and we were still having a great time together. Luke had met my parents, and I had met his. They invited me for dinner at their house that Sunday. I was so excited to have a bit of bonding time with his family. That Sunday we were having a good time at dinner.

After we had finished dinner, I went to use the toilet in the hall. But I overheard Luke's ma and da asking him if he liked me.

Luke said: 'Yeah, course I do. She's a lovely girl.'

'Well, your father and I just think you could find someone a bit better and nicer for a girlfriend,' I heard Luke's ma say.

Luke let off a big roar.

'What are you talking about? I really like Megan, no matter what you say. You won't stop me from seeing her!'

I was in shock. I pretended I hadn't heard what was said, but I didn't say much for the rest of the afternoon. No one else did either, at the table.

Later that evening Luke told me about what his ma and da said to him about me. I acted like I hadn't heard the conversation. But Luke had said to me not to mind them, and that nothing would split us up.

We were only seeing each other that short while, but Luke and I were in love with each other.

And then months had passed and we were still together.

One Saturday morning, Luke rang me up.

'Megan, I have bad news. I just had the biggest fight with my ma and da.'

I told Luke he could come up to my house for a few hours and I met him at the bus stop near my house. He seemed very annoyed, and I kept wondering what was going on.

We went up to my room and Luke sat me down. 'It's not just the fight,' said Luke. 'There's more.'

I started to panic. 'Why? What's wrong?'

'My ma and da just told me that we're moving to England. My da got a job over there as a teacher.'

My face dropped. The only thing I could think of was, *Luke is going to leave me. Luke is going to leave me.*

I tried to act calm, and quietly asked Luke did he have to go too.

'They told me I've no choice.'

It felt like the tears were going to drop from my eyes. I had such a big lump in my throat. I was trying to hold the tears in.

Luke was going to England in two weeks.

Luke stayed with me for the whole day. That night his da had to come to my house to collect him. I didn't even walk Luke out to the door, I was that annoyed. I didn't want to see his da! I knew Luke's parents didn't like me, but I never thought in a million years that they would take him away from me.

Luke went home and I couldn't help but cry. Later that night I was talking to Luke on the phone. We both couldn't believe that he was leaving in two weeks.

'Maybe it won't be as bad as we think. I will come over and visit you on all the breaks from school, even at Christmas!'

I told him I had spoken to my ma, and she said I could visit him too.

'See, Megan, it'll be grand.'

And I started to think, well…*maybe it won't be so bad.* Luke and I had two weeks left with each other and we made the best of it.

****

On the day Luke was to leave, I went down to his house to say goodbye to him.

I was so confused because Luke had told me that there was talk about me that his parents had heard, but they wouldn't tell him what.

I'd never done anything ever to hurt Luke. I loved him so much. He was getting ready to go, but then he started crying. And that set me off. He told me he loved me, and that he would never let me go.

'Promise me that, Luke.'

'I promise,' he said. And then he left.

Luke had set a date to come back and visit me, so that was all I could wait for.

****

Luke and I continued to write to each other. He had meant to come over and visit me at Christmas, but he wasn't allowed. So we just kept writing to each other and talking on the phone.

My feelings for Luke were kind of dipping, because I had not seen him in ages. It was very hard, but my best friend Karl was always there to help me through it. Even though Karl was a friend, I didn't fancy him. He wasn't Luke.

And suddenly Luke was coming over – he rang me and told me he was going to visit relations in Ireland. I was delighted and I couldn't wait to see him.

He came over the following Thursday and I spent all weekend with him, and I fell more and more in love with him than ever. And then it was Monday morning and he had to go home.

I was so upset. But he told me he would be back over in a month.

****

I was waiting on Luke to write to me but he didn't. I wrote to him, but he never wrote back.

I kept writing and writing for about a month, but still I got no reply. Karl helped me through it. Karl and I began to get closer and closer; he got on very well with my parents and his parents loved me. But he still wasn't Luke.

Then I started to forget about Luke and get over him.

But I fell for Karl instead.

****

And then a whole year had passed since I'd last heard from Luke. Karl and I were now in love with each other.

Out of the blue one day Luke called, and I just said, 'Don't ring here again,' and hung up.

I'm so happy with my life now. Karl's parents love me, and he treats me like a princess. I thought I loved Luke. But in the end, it was my best friend I loved instead.

Paula's Story
Klaudia Bucka

Hi, my name is Paula and I come from Spain, but I'm Polish. When my parents were eighteen years old they ran away from Poland to Spain, where they stayed. I love my country. I am fifteen years old and I'm blonde with blue eyes. I have two friends – Rosa and Lola. I'm popular at school and I think everyone cares about them as well. I have chosen a wedding dress (I saw it in a magazine and I thought, 'This is it.') I love photography. My parents are rich and my life is…perfect.

13 July 2009

Parents want to talk with me tomorrow.

15 July 2009

What? They want to move! MOVE! Where? To London! OMG. I don't know where it is on the map. Next week…They bought the house for my birthday, yes…dream present.

1 September 2009

First day in new school. I'm must wake up at 6.30 a.m.! I dress in new, ugly clothes and go to the bus stop, where there was a big yellow bus. He waits for me. School is horrible, everything in sad colours; no pink, no yellow, no orange, no red. Just green, grey and dark blue. People here are so nice; maybe too nice? In school I can see the group: football boys and, of course, Barbie girls. Just one group is the most interesting. There are five people: three girls and two boys. They talk only with each other. They have a strange style of dress. They stand out among the others, but not too much. On their faces you can see an incredible calmness and composure. They made a huge impression on me. One hour later I go home...Lovely.

16 September 2009

Tomorrow is my birthday. At lunchtime I don't sit with anyone. All the time I'm looking at them. The girls with their big green eyes and the boys' blue ones are so amazing.

17 September 2009

Mom and Dad bought ticket to London for Rosa and Lola, just for my birthday party! I can't believe it. Also they bought me a new computer, a Nikon camera, and pictures for my own living room. Nothing special. My party was in a new club. There were not too many people, but I had good time – the best I have had in the last month.

9 October 2009

I see a new boy in class. He also has blue big eyes. My first thoughts are: He must be one of 'them'. And I was right. His name is Nathan. The others are called Kate, Louise, Samantha, Adam and David.

17 October 2009

I cannot believe it! I wanted to play with my new camera so I decided to go to a park, and I found a kind of bunker. And what is even better, I met Adam – one of 'them'. He had the same facial expression as I had when he saw me. With a funny voice, he said, 'Hi.' I started to laugh. I was so shocked. He had to take pictures for his photography homework. It turned out that he was really nice. We chatted for hours. Adam has a great knowledge of cameras. After this interesting day he walked me home.

18 October 2009

It is 3 a.m. My parents woke me and had the greatest news for me. I'm flying to Spain, on

Monday! Again, I cannot believe what is happening. This year is really different. Unfortunately I cannot take you with me, Dear Diary, because my grandma will be very interested in what is in your pages. I will write on the Monday after I return! Kisses.

23 October 2009

It was brilliant! In Spain, it is hot, even at this time of year. I love this climate and this country. Everything is perfect. My cousins grew up here and I regret that I was not with them – or, actually, with the rest of my family. Only after arriving I realised how much I missed them and still miss them.

Of course, in London rain welcomed me home. But I have bigger things on my mind. Adam says that no one can know that we meet. Terribly sorry but cannot tell anyone.

24 October 2009

I still think about Adam. Why are we secret? He knows how good we are talking with each other, as it is fun and interesting. Sometime our relationship can be revealed...I hope...

27 October 2009

Just as I thought. Adam came to me and just said that I did not ask for anything. For the first time ever we were fighting and interrupting each other. But I see too that he is hiding a secret. I just feel that I want to say something, but cannot. He needs time.

17 November 2009

Things have changed. Now I sit with 'them' at lunchtime. It is strange...different. But I like it. They all have much to say and are terribly intelligent. I start to like this school and London because Adam showed me another side of life here.

When my parents and Anna (the maid) had gone to sleep, he came to me and began knocking on the door of my balcony. He said he wanted to take me on a trip. It was crazy. We went to a bar and someone wanted to share a beer with us. What a miracle...We got the London Eye for free. Adam has a car, too – a good thing, ha ha :) Now I know what 'I love my life' means. You have to feel it! I'm so happy. I'm not thinking about Spain so much these days. We could definitely do this again.

19 November 2009

Nathan still does not like me. Everyone else does, except him. I talked about this with Adam and he told me not to worry. He took me to the movies for a horror film. Never again!

20 November 2009

Today was supposed to be a normal day. We went to Kate's house. Today was supposed to be a day like any other. But it was not. They want to talk to me, but only in private. So we have all locked ourselves in a room with Kate. They start to tell me about some books, and I believe the person who is in the story is a vampire. And then I realise…and I am speechless.

They are vampires.

'That is why we have such eyes, and we never mature.'

They are strange…

25 November 2009

They said that because one of them loves me they want me to be 'one of them'.

29 November 2009

Too much information. I don't understand…I cannot write about it.

24 December 2009

Merry Christmas and Happy New Year.

11 January 2010

We went back to school after Christmas break. Adam is now my best friend. Rosa and Lola forgot about me. They have a world of shopping malls, the latest phones and best events. Now I am glad I'm not like them: 'normal'.

16 January 2010

Tuesday. I dislike Tuesdays.

18 February 2010

Today we all met in the park. We went on the swings. It was after seven o'clock and there was a small child playing.

They wanted to know everything about me. What? Where? How? Why?

23 February 2010

David and Louise are together. It's all strange and difficult to understand, because if 'this type' of people are together they are stronger. I don't know how to say it…They complement each other.

10 March 2010

Today is Kate's birthday. I did not buy anything big. When I walked around the shops I saw a beautiful little jewellery box in the Gothic style. I hope she likes it.

17 March 2010

For some time, but not for too long, I talk with Adam. I do not know what's happening. 'You no longer come to me. We don't watch movies together, we don't go for walks and we don't do the trips anymore,' I complain. He doesn't seem to care.

18 March 2010

I do not believe what is happening. Adam came to me after such a long time and he took me for a long walk. He bought me a huge bouquet of flowers and explained everything. Exactly.

'We are already together quite a long time and I trust you completely. I still remember your first day at school. I like that we met in the park. It was really nice. And probably for good because…'

19 March 2010

He…He loves me.

20 March 2010

But can he really? But it is not possible! Wow. After all, he is not a man.

They are in pairs. Everyone has someone. They should be together. This cannot be. That was not what I was expecting. I do not know what to do. I do not know what to say. I do not know. I'd prefer…I'd prefer…

22 March 2010

Today on my windowsill by my bed lay a small blue box. Inside it, a narrow silver bracelet with a tiny little heart…

23 March 2010

I say, 'Yes.'

31 March 2010

Was funny to see the scene in school when I was with Adam. As a couple. Still, I cannot get used to it. I feel rather stupid. The worst was from Kate because of her friendship. She was the first to see my new bracelet.

8 April 2010

I feel like an idiot. I was at Kate's home – with everyone. On Adam's jacket I found some short red hair. I thought, oh no! For the rest of the day I pretended that everything was okay. But after parting from Adam I hid, watching him with Kate, on the way to his house. But he went to the nearest bus stop and she did not get on the bus when it came. The red-haired girl turned out to be his aunt…

10 April 2010

Today it rains all day.

11 April 2010

Walk with Adam.

13 April 2010

Watching film with Adam.

17 April 2010

I love spending time with him.

19 April 2010

I love to receive flowers from him.

26 May 2010

Last day of school. HOLIDAYS!

27 May 2010

It was a beautiful evening. We went for a walk, as always along the same avenues, but with an awkward silence – as never before. At last we came to the tree on which with a knife he once wrote 'Paula and Adam Forever'. It was our tree. Our favourite, because when you sat under it you could see the beautiful meadow. Adam grabbed my hand and said that he loves me. He loves me but we cannot be together.

What?

1 June 2010

I ran away. I ran away because what can I do? I ran to my house. I buy a ticket. I'm in Spain. I do not know if this is still my home. Every day I talk for hours with my grandmother. She tells my parents I am staying. I do not believe. I just do not believe what has happened. I do not care if my parents miss me. We came to London almost a year ago, and my friends have forgotten about me. I've had enough.

3 June 2010

Once I loved the heat. The Spanish weather. And now I miss the rain in London. I did not think that I would ever miss those grey days, but I loved to sit in bed with hot chocolate and a good book.

5 June 2010

I still wonder what might happen at school, how our Barbie girls are. Are they constantly analysing what happened?

6 June 2010

Why did he say that? Why did she leave?

8 June 2010

Today my grandmother and I baked a cake. I felt like a five-year-old child. I am glad I approached her. It was awfully smart of me. I would like to know half as much as she does. But I still don't know what to do now…

11 June 2010

I spend most evenings with my iPhone listening to some sad songs. Oh, what's wrong with me? I return to London.

1 July 2010

A month has passed – no one has visited me.

2 July 2010

Kate arrives unexpectedly. To cxplain everything to me, she says. She keeps it as short as possible. I'm just an ordinary person. It is unheard of that what happened to me could happen. But they want me to be one of them. This time literally. There is no other way. If I loved him, really loved – I would. But can I? Grandmother told me that I need to follow my heart, and I think I'll just do it.

4 July 2010

When I saw Adam I could not resist him. I did not think that it was possible for someone to be so deeply missed. I cannot believe that I walked with him through the streets like we did before. I do not really know if I'm ready for what I'm going to do, but now I feel it. I feel that I love him.

11 July 2010

A year has passed since I started writing this diary. My life has changed 360 degrees. I never thought I would meet someone so fascinating and that I would move somewhere so far away from Spain. But I think it did me good. Now I know where my home is…with Adam. I don't need anything more.

Help!

Megan Burke

Louise grew up in Ballymun, in a place called Balcurris. She moved to Ballymun with her ma and da when she was just three years old. Her ma and da were both alcoholics. They didn't really look after Louise properly, so at the age of nine she was put into foster care. She moved to Swords to live with her foster parents, but was very lonely.

When Louise was thirteen years old she started secondary school. She made a few friends in the school. Then she started hanging around with a group of girls outside school. These girls were always out with boys much older than them; they drank alcohol and took drugs every weekend. Louise wanted to fit in with all her new friends, as she thought that everything they did was cool. She started to drink a lot of alcohol and stopped going home at the weekends. Louise didn't care what her foster parents would say or do. She went a bit mad once she started drinking. When Louise would go home at all hours of the morning her foster parents would be up waiting for her.

'Where were you?'

'Never mind. I was out with my friends,' Louise always replied.

They tried to ground her, but she didn't take any notice. She used to just sneak out her bedroom window.

Louise's behaviour went on like this for two years, and continued to get worse. She started to smoke cigarettes and cannabis and gave her foster parents an awful time. At the age of fifteen Louise was brought home by the gardaí after being caught robbing lots of alcohol.

Her foster parents were devastated by what Louise had done. They just couldn't control what she did anymore. They had tried everything. They sat down and talked to her. They got her social worker to talk to her. They tried grounding her. They tried to keep her away from the group of people she hung out with. But nothing worked. When they asked her to stop this out-of-control behaviour Louise would say, 'Never mind what I do. It's nothing got to do with you what I do. Keep your nose out of my business!'

Louise stopped turning up for school some mornings. She would mitch off and go into town, to all the older boys she hung out with. She was due to sit her Junior Cert. Her grades in school had dropped, but she didn't care. Things got worse and Louise started to take drugs like cocaine. She took these drugs when she went drinking at the weekends. But it got further out of hand and she started to drink during the week. When she wouldn't come home her foster parents would ring the guards. They were sick of sitting up worried about where she was and what she was doing.

When her foster parents realised she was doing drugs, they tried telling her how dangerous it was. She would just laugh at them and say, 'Shut up, will you? I'm not a baby. I'm sixteen now.'

Louise had been in trouble with the guards lots of times, and she didn't care. She got into a relationship with a twenty-one-year old, and she was just sixteen. Her fella, John, took drugs a lot of the time too. He also dealt drugs. Louise started to have sex with her fella, because that's what he wanted. She lost all respect for herself. Louise caught STDs off her fella and still didn't care. A few months into their relationship, her fella became violent towards her as he was always on drugs.

Louise thought she was in love. But she was still young and didn't even know what love was. All of her friends copped on to themselves and started to go to school. They wanted to do well for themselves. Her friends told her to get away from her fella, as things would only get worse. But she didn't listen. She thought her friends were jealous because she had a boyfriend and they didn't. Louise grew more distant from her friends. She just wanted to be with John. Her foster parents didn't know that Louise had a fella who was much older than her. Louise used to sneak out of her house at all hours of the morning to go visit him. They both became addicted to cocaine. They wanted it all of the time.

Louise was still just sixteen when she fell pregnant. When John found out he didn't want the baby. But Louise was keeping it. John said he didn't care what she did. It was nothing to do with him. He went off to have sex with other girls. He didn't care what she thought.

Louise was now completely out of control and her foster parents didn't want her living with them. They disowned her once they found out she was on gear. There was nothing to help her, as she didn't want help. The guards were rung for her all of the time, as she wouldn't come home. Her friends didn't know where she was either. Her friends couldn't even help her. There was just no talking to Louise at this stage.

Louise became homeless after just turning seventeen. She was staying in hostels night after night, with no money or no clean clothes. Sometimes she was with John; sometimes she wasn't. He had no money either as he was in debt over the drugs he was selling. But they needed money. They were expecting a child!

They started to beg on the street as their families turned their backs on them. Things got worse for Louise when John started to beat her up all of the time. It was like he had nothing better to be doing. Louise got in touch with her social worker. They gave her somewhere to stay while she was pregnant. Louise still went out to visit John, as he was still homeless. They still took gear.

One afternoon Louise went into town, to John, as she needed gear. He was so out of his head on his drugs that he beat Louise worse than ever before. He left her black and blue and full of blood and he left her on the side of the street. She was heavily pregnant at this stage. Some girl ran over to her screaming, 'Are you OK?'

Panicking, she called an ambulance as Louise was badly injured. The hospital helped Louise and she stayed overnight, as they needed to make sure the baby was safe. The hospital offered to help Louise, and her baby, to stay off drugs. Louise went into rehab for the rest of her pregnancy.

Louise gave birth to a beautiful baby girl called Abby. Three years on, Louise is away from drugs and will do anything for her daughter. She is back living with her foster parents. Louise has not heard from John, and doesn't want to as he is still on drugs. She does not want her baby growing up around drugs. Maybe when Abby is old enough she will tell her who her father is.

Junior Night
Hughie Collins

I'll tell you a little story, so relax and enjoy. It's about me and my life and the time I went out with Patrick and Hughie for Junior Night. Don't know what Junior Night is? You get your Junior Cert exam results and straight away forget about them by having the biggest party of the year.

My name is Michael Collins. I'm named after the other Michael Collins, who you might have heard of. I live in Fairview House, and hang around with my two cousins Patrick and Hughie and well…well, there's not much else to say about me. So I'll just get on with the story.

On Junior Night we went down town. We were crossing the Belcamp Road – me, Hughie and Patrick – showing off, acting the prick, you know? Real cool, and all. We thought we were, anyway. We were running out and stopping the cars in the middle of the road, just so we could cross the street. We stepped out in front of a car, and a bus came flying, but we didn't see it and we nearly all got knocked down. I jumped forwards, Hughie jumped backwards, and Hughie got his leg hit by another car. He was shook up after that, but I just laughed my head off.

After that we were starving, so we went to Stan's restaurant in town, where they serve burgers and chips, and beer too. We were there ordering food and drinks and having a good time until a few wasted boys came over to us, and started staring us down. Their looks told us we weren't welcome, and I didn't want trouble. But Patrick gave them a bit of lip, and suddenly they were laying into us. Stan, the owner of the restaurant, jumped in, and threw us into the street. So the fight just went on outside, or at least it did until the guards showed up and we all scarpered.

They chased us, but not for long. We were too fast – even though Hughie had a dead leg from the car and my nose was bleeding like crazy from the fight. Later on we went to Quie's Niteclub, and tried to get in, but the bouncers wouldn't let us in because we were too young and my shirt was covered in blood. Patrick called the bouncer a baldy prick, but that didn't help. So we just hung around outside the club for a while. Then Hughie flung a rock at the bouncer and we legged it.

Hughie got a phone call saying there was a party on in Coolock, so we said:

'OK, let's go for a while.'

I had a bad feeling about it. Hughie's mates are a bunch of robbing, junkie wasters. But along I went anyway. The party was lame, but there was loads of alcohol, so we stayed for a while.

I might have stayed all night, but some lad at the party lobbed a petrol bomb into a house down the road and the whole thing went up. I heard it was because of some argument over a girl. Hughie's mates are all nut jobs.

'Enough is enough,' I said and I told the boys I was going home.

Patrick and Hughie said they were staying.

'Are you sure?'

'Yes.'

I split and got a taxi.

The next day I got up out of bed and called in for Patrick. His mam said that he hadn't come back last night, and that he'd stayed in Hughie's.

I said, 'Ok. Thanks.'

I went to call in for Hughie. His da, Hughie Senior, said neither of the lads had come back last night, and that Hughie was supposed to be at Patrick's. Hughie Senior called the guards.

I called Martin, one of the guys from the party the night before, and he told me that Patrick and Hughie went off with a few dangerous fellas. Martin said, 'I tried to stop them, but they wouldn't listen to me.'

I didn't tell Hughie or Patrick's parents about this part. It didn't matter because, two hours later, Hughie's mam, Bridget, rang me and said the guards had found Hughie in a car on the main road.

The car had been badly shot up, according to the guards. There were rounds fired and a few people had been hurt. All of them had been transferred to Dhúlaigh Hospital. Bridget asked me to come to the hospital. We sat in the waiting area – me, Hughie's mam and Hughie Senior.

The doctor came in after a while and said that Hughie was in a coma. Hughie's mam asked, 'How long until he wakes up?'

The doctor said that he didn't know.

After three hours and twenty-three minutes, the doctor came around and said to Bridget and Hughie Senior that Hughie was coming on better than he had hoped for.

'Is he awake yet?' asked Hughie's mam.

The doctor said he wasn't. Then he told them that Hughie had tested positive for cocaine and cannabis. Hughie's mam and da said that that wasn't possible.

The doctor said, 'I'm sorry. Even though it's hard to hear, the facts are the facts.'

Hughie Senior was furious at the doctor. Hughie's da is pretty scary when he's mad. It was around then that Patrick texted me. He'd run off before the car had been attacked, and he'd been hiding. But I didn't want to speak to him.

Hughie stayed in a coma.

The guards got in touch with Hughie's parents over the next few days, and told his mam that the other three fellas in the car were drug dealers – well, two of them were, anyway. And they owed money to other people for drugs. That's why the car was shot at. Hughie's ma asked the guards to catch the people who did it. The guards said they were looking into it, and they'd found fingerprints on the bullet casing at the scene. So that was good.

It was weeks later when Hughie's mam called me and said that Hughie was waking up. They'd all rushed to the hospital as soon as they'd got the call from the doctors. I think Hughie's mam was upset that she hadn't been there. Hughie Senior was crying, he was so happy. The funny thing about it was that Hughie had been in a coma for six weeks by then, but he still thought that it was the morning after Junior Night.

The Fight Life

Gary Duffy

1

Andrew is a hard-working man with a horrible life. He doesn't know why he works when he is treated like shit by his boss and workmates. Andrew was walking through an alleyway when he heard the noise of grunting futher up the alley. It was two men fighting with blood all over them and a big crowd of people around them. He walked further up to the crowd and cut through them to the front.

He turned his head and asked the guy next to him, 'What's going on? Why are they fighting?'

'They're fighting for money,' the man said to him.

'What money?' Andrew asked.

'It's a street fight. If you want you can fight after them, but you don't get money.'

Andrew paused while one of the men fighting gave a punch to the other, making him turn around, spitting out a lot of blood. The blood went all over Andrew. Andrew said: 'Sure, why not? I'm already covered in blood.'

The man turned with his hand open for a handshake. 'I'm Jamie. I organise tournaments and street fights. You want to see a fight, you come to me. You want to fight, you come to me.'

'Well, if I do good in the fight, I just might give you a call,' Andrew said with a smirk. He shook his hand. 'The name is Andrew.'

After the fight Andrew took his tie and shirt off. Then he went into the circle that was formed by the crowd of people. Out of the crowd came a skinny, bony man with his fists put up.

Andrew smiled and thought to himself, *This should be easy enough.*

The opponent threw his left fist as hard as he could and punched out Andrew's tooth. Andrew was shocked that he could hit that hard. Andrew kneed the skinny man in the stomach and winded him. They both started exchanging punches until Andrew headbutted his opponent. The man gave in and stood up to shake Andrew's hand. 'Well done. It was a good fight.'

Andrew shook his hand. 'Thanks, it was my first.'

Jamie ran up to him, cheering with the crowd along with him.

'Great fight,' said Jamie. 'You going to fight again?'

'I'll think about it,' Andrew said and walked around the corner.

2

It had been two weeks since the fight and Andrew couldn't get it out of his head. He walked by a restaurant where Jamie, the man Andrew met in the alley, was eating and talking to two other people. Jamie saw Andrew walking by the open windows of the restaurant and shouted his name as he ran out of the restaurant. Andrew quickly turned around and, without any hesitation, remembered Jamie's name. Jamie asked him how he was doing and Andrew said, 'I'm all right. I just can't stop thinking about that fight.'

Jamie smiled and said, 'Come here. I have two people I want you to meet.' Andrew was confused but went with him. They went to the table where the two men were eating. Jamie introduced Andrew to the two men.

'Andrew, this is Sean and Bob,' said Jamie. 'Bob is a street fighter who hasn't lost a fight so far and Sean is his manager.'

'Nice to meet you,' Andrew said.

'We were just talking about you,' said Sean.

'Yeah, Jamie was telling us about how you won your fight two weeks ago,' said Bob.

'It was nothing. He was skinny and bony,' Andrew smirked.

'Nonsense. It doesn't matter if you're fat or skinny, small or tall. It's all about speed, strength and who can take the most damage withoug giving up.' Andrew nodded along with what Bob was saying.

'I agree. As long as you have speed and strength, you could win a lot of fights,' Sean told him. 'You should fight in the upcoming tournament that Jamie is setting up.'

'Yeah, I don't see why not,' Jamie said to Bob and Sean. 'I'll see you later.' Jamie walked out with Andrew behind him.

'So, what's with this tournament?' Andrew asked.

'What do you mean, what's with this tournament? It's a tournament to fight in and get some money.'

'Do you think I could win?' Andrew stopped walking.

'You could but you need to start hitting the gym and fight more,' Jamie replied. 'The tournament is not for six months. I'll set up fights for you. Is that OK?'

'Yeah sure,' Andrew replied, 'that would be great.'

3

Jamie put Andrew in a fight every two weeks and he won most of the time. Andrew went to the gym every second day. He punched and kicked the punching bags, lifted weights and started eating healthily and drank a protein shake every day. After the fights he would walk into work with black eyes, a busted nose and missing teeth. All his colleagues would stop working and look at him while whispering to each other. His boss would say, 'Good God, man; what happened to you?' Every time Andrew would have an excuse: he fell down the stairs, got hopped on by a gang or got into a bar fight, but he would not tell him that he was in an illegal fight club.

After three months, Jamie and Andrew became good friends. They both started talking in Jamie's apartment, and Andrew said, 'Why don't I live here?'

Jamie laughed. 'Because I live here.'

'No, seriously. Why don't I live here with you until after the tournament?' Jamie thought about it and agreed.

'It would be easier than walking over to you to go to the gym. I don't see why not.' So Andrew moved into the apartment. He packed all his stuff and Jamie helped him carry it to his apartment. When Andrew was bringing a heavy box up, he meet a girl on the stairs.

'Hi. Do I know you?' she asked.

'No, you don't; but you could. The name's Andrew,' he said. 'And you are?'

'My name is Kim. Nice to meet you.'

'Nice to meet you too,' said Andrew.

'Are you new in the building?' Kim asked.

'Yeah, I'm moving in with Jamie. Do you know him?'

Yeah, I do. Listen I've got to go; I'm in a rush.'

'Yeah, OK. I hope to see you again.'

A week later Andew met Kim again and asked her out on a date.

Kim said, 'Yeah, I'd love to.'

'Great. This Saturday then around eight o'clock.'

'Yeah, I'm free then,' replied Kim. They went to a nice restaurant. They didn't get home until 1 a.m. They both had a lot of fun.

Weeks went by and Andrew was still going to the gym and still going out with Kim. A week before the tournament, Andrew suddenly had his doubts about it and was afraid. He kept saying, 'Can I win this? I don't think I can win.' He kept repeating this over and over. Jamie assured him that he could and would win. A week later he was still worried and his first fight was about to start.

Jamie said to him, 'You wouldn't want Kim to see you worried like this if she were here.'

'Well she ain't here,' Andrew said.

'And why is that?' asked Jamie. 'Why didn't you ask her to come?'

'I didn't ask her because she doesn't know I fight.'

'Why didn't you tell her?' Jamie asked.

'She might not like me if I told her about it.'

'Well, you can't keep lying about it.'

'Yeah, I know.'

'Anyway, your first fight is starting in ten minutes.'

4

The first fight was about to begin and it was the start of the tournament. Andrew had never been this nervous before. Andrew looked to the audience and noticed Sean and Bob, the two men he had met in the restaurant. The opponent on the other side was very tall and looked as if he could take more than a couple of punches. The bell rang and they both circled around the ring. Andrew threw the first punch but the opponent dodged it and punched Andrew instead. Andrew shucked it off and kicked the man in the chest. He was winded and wrapped his hands around his chest. Andrew took this to his advantage and started boxing as hard and fast as he could. The opponent pushed Andrew away and he took the time to catch his breath. Andrew kept punching while the other man was blocking. After a while Andrew connected with a nice uppercut to the jaw and knocked the opponent out. He had won the first fight of the tournament and there were three more fights until the next round.

Bob went over to Andrew and smiled at him, 'Good fight,' Bob said.

Andrew said, 'Thanks. Can't wait till I see your fight.'

'Well, it's after these two fights so I can't wait either.'

Two fights later and Bob's fight was about to begin. The bell rang and he just walked over to his opponent and knocked him out with one punch. Andrew and Jamie were shocked. They couldn't believe what they had just seen.

Andrew walked over to Bob and said, 'That was a nice punch. Well done.'

'Thanks; it was too easy.'

The second round was about to begin and Andrew's fight was just about to start. Jamie kept saying, 'You can do this, you can do this.' Andrew took a bottle of water and drank the whole thing. Jamie said to him, 'Get ready; it starts in a minute.' Andrew went into the ring and faced his opponent. The bell rang and the opponent ran at

Andrew, kicked him and pushed Andrew back. Andrew then threw a punch and landed it on his nose and busted it. The opponent saw the blood and went mad. He started throwing kicks, but Andrew was blocking them. Andrew threw another and his opponent fell. Then he gave up and Andrew won. The second round was done and all that was left was Bob's fight. If Bob won this then he would face Andrew in the finals.

Sean, who was Bob's manager, was telling Bob that he could win and that he would be facing Andrew when he won this fight. The bell rang and Bob's fight began. They both started punching each other non-stop until Bob's opponent got tired. Bob kicked him in the ribs and made him fall to his knees and then finished him with a punch. The opponent fell to the ground while Bob walked over to his manager. Sean gave him a bottle of water and Bob drank it in one gulp. Jamie walked around and told everyone the final start would be in two hours for the fighters to freshen up a bit.

5

Andrew and Bob's fight was starting in two hours and Andrew just wanted to eat. He went to a shop and bought a roll, while Bob went to sleep and Sean went to the shop. Andrew met Sean and they both starting talking about the tournament. Andrew asked Sean, 'Do you think I've got a chance to win?'

Sean replied, 'Maybe. You're becoming a better fighter every match, so, yeah, I think so.' Andrew said thanks and walked out of the shop.

Two hours later the fight was about to begin. Andrew and Bob stood across from each other ready to fight. They were both nervous. The bell rang and they both circled. Bob threw the first punch and hit Andrew in the stomach, then Andrew punched Bob in the jaw. They kept exchanging punches as hard as they could. After five minutes of it they were extremely tired and couldn't keep their fists up. They were both gasping for air, then Andrew went in with a fist and got Bob in the chin. Bob hit Andrew in the nose. Andrew kicked Bob in the leg and made him fall to his knees. Bob couldn't stand up. Andrew stood there waiting. After two minutes Bob got to his feet and Andrew punched him in the nose. It started to bleed. Bob punched Andrew in the mouth and knocked out a tooth. Andrew hit Bob in the stomach and then hit him again in the jaw. Bob fell, and this time he couldn't get up. The bell rang and it was all over. Andrew had won the tournament. He put his hands in the air and fell on his back.

Thirty minutes later Andrew woke up.

'Congratulations on the win,' Jamie said.

'What win?' asked Andrew.

'The tournament; you won it,' answered Jamie.

Andrew asked about Bob, and then he came into the room. 'I'm OK. You deserved to win. It was a great fight.'

'Thanks,' said Andrew.

Bob asked, 'So, are you going to do the next tournament?'

Andrew paused and thought for a few seconds, then he replied: 'Nah, I'm not going to fight anymore.'

'Are you sure?' asked Jamie.

'Yeah, I'm sure,' answered Andrew.

Andrew got up and left. He still talked to Jamie and hung around with him, but he never fought again. At work he was treated better. He had a better life and he had Kim as his girlfriend.

The Perfect Ending... Or Is It?

Eve Gibney

Brooke and her friend Fee were walking through a market in the South of France. Brooke had bags up to her elbows full of dresses and shoes. She and her friend were feeling exhausted, but they kept on going with the shopping. Brooke bumped into a man.

'Oh Jesus! Sorry!'

Brooke double-looked the man who then gave her a huge grin.

She said: 'Heya! I don't think you're from around here.'

'Well, by the redness of me arms – no…'

'Well, you're a northsider anyways.'

'Ah yeah – I'm from Ballymun. What about yourself?'

'Only down the road in Coolock, so I am. Mad or what?

'What's your name?'

'Brooke – yours?'

'Mine's Cian. I may as well give ya me number, love. Yar quite a cracker!'

Brooke went really scarlet. She took his number then gave him hers. They were about to go their separate ways when Cian goes: 'I'll text ya next week when we're home.'

Cian did text Brooke. 'Hey! Do you want to go the pictures Friday night?'

Brooke texted him back: 'Yeah sure, why not? I'm not up to anything :)'

Brooke and Cian started going out together and found they had a lot in common. They both liked socialising with their friends at the weekends and both loved R&B and hip-hop music. For their first anniversary they decided to go on a trip to Paris.

It was a warm summer evening. They were in a restaurant alongside the River Seine. The restaurant was posh. The tables were covered in white linen table cloths and shining silver cutlery with a centre-piece of red roses. They had just finished their starter when Cian started rooting in his pocket. He then got down on one knee and said, 'Brooke – will ya marry me?'

Brooke screamed with delight.

'Yes!'

No sooner than had they got off the plane than Brooke began organising the wedding she had dreamed of since she was a child. She wanted the big white dress, the diamante tiara, the pink rose petals scattered down the aisle of the old grey stone church, with his and her families there watching them.

Finally, the day she dreamed of arrived. The house was buzzing with atmosphere. It was packed with her aunties, her sisters and family friends. Brooke was not long up out of her bed. She was in her blue polka dot pyjamas and her hair was up in a bun. She was about to get her make-up done when her sister heard the doorbell. It was Cian. He asked if he could talk to Brooke, so she decided to go upstairs to her childhood bedroom.

This was where her worst nightmare came true. Cian began with a trembling stutter.

'I–I can't go through with this.'

'Ha ha! Aren't you funny!'

'Brooke, I'm being serious. Sit down, will ya?'

'Right…'

'This is not what I want. I don't want to be settled down and have kids at this age. I want to go travelling and make the most of my young years.'

Brooke broke down and sat there bawling.

'I'm sorry.'

Cian stood there with the saddest face Brooke had never seen. A tear appeared in his eyes and he left. Brooke sat there on the bed staring out the window for hours.

What was she going to do?

Brooke had had their lives practically planned out. She thought she wouldn't be able to cope without what she thought was the perfect life. But she ended up going to college where she studied photography and became a wedding photographer. She became a well-known photographer and now she is always doing weddings.

She has just done a big wedding and sits looking at the photographs. She sees a picture of a beautiful bride and groom. They look so happy together. There's a picture of them standing outside a beautiful church on a summer day with all of their families, smiling and laughing. Brooke thinks to herself that the atmosphere reminds her of that morning in her mother's kitchen and what was meant to be the most special day of her life. Now, Brooke knows that maybe the whole traditional wedding thing wasn't meant for her.

So she gets all glammed up and ready for a night on the tiles with her good college friends.

Today, Tomorrow, Forever?

Sarah Gorry

'Get up Alex!'

Alex moaned and pulled the duvet over her head. Her best friend, Ciara, was throwing things at her now.

'Alex, if you don't get up I'm going to throw the radio at you!'

Alex jumped up, as Ciara was the kind of person who *would* throw a radio at you. She looked at her phone: **one new message** was showing on the screen. It was from Kyle. Kyle was Alex's ex-boyfriend who had broken up with her just a week ago. The message had been sent when he was drunk. He always said things that he didn't mean when he was drunk. It was hard to make out with all the bad spelling. Alex gave up on trying to read it and deleted it.

'Ciara, do you want to go to the cinema this Saturday, to get my mind off Kyle?'

'Sure, but do you mind if Shane comes?'

Shane was Ciara's boyfriend of two years. Shane and Alex never got along but they had to try and pretend they did.

'Of course not, we can go see that new horror movie that's out.'

Alex got out of bed and started getting ready for school. She lifted the straightener to her hair. Alex had wild, curly hair but never liked it. It looked odd with her pale face and green eyes. She spent forty minutes every morning doing her hair. When she'd finished her hair, she started her make-up. She didn't wear much, just eyeliner and mascara and sometimes blush. Alex looked at the clock. It was nine forty-five, and if she didn't leave now she'd be late. Again.

'Can you ever be early?' Ciara laughed.

'I could, but I love my bed too much,' Alex told her as she rushed down the stairs. They hurried to school, which, luckily, was only around the corner. Their friend Orla was waiting at the gate, tapping her foot impatiently.

'Where have you been?' Orla asked as they rushed up to her. 'I have been waiting here for fifteen minutes and Mr Timmons is giving anyone who's late detention for two weeks!' Orla was very uptight. She hated being late or getting into trouble at all. She was the reason none of them got into trouble.

'Calm down, Orla. We still have three minutes until the bell goes.' They rushed into the school and got to class just as the bell rang.

The day went as any other day would go: classes, teachers, writing and whatever else you're meant to do in school. When they were walking out of school Alex noticed Kyle at the gate. He was sitting on the wall, staring right at her. He walked over and tried to hug her, but she pushed him away.

'Why are you here?' she asked, looking at the ground.

'I'm here to see you. I want to apologise.' Alex was still looking at the ground. She knew that if she looked up she'd burst into tears.

'Apologise for what?' She tried to ignore the ball in her throat. She was clutching Ciara's arm, making sure she didn't leave her.

'You know what I want to apologise for. Last week.' He was staring at her. She could feel his eyes on her.

'I miss you, Alex.' Alex couldn't talk. She let go of Ciara's arm. Ciara looked at her and walked away with Orla.

'I'm sorry,' he said, his eyes still fixed on Alex. 'I didn't mean it; I really do love you, Alex.'

'I'm sorry too. I shouldn't have acted so childish.'

'It's okay. Do you want to try again?' He smiled.

Alex looked up. 'Of course.' She hugged him.

Kyle walked Alex home and kissed her goodnight. By then it was already past six and it was dark. As soon as she went inside she got a text from Kyle. It read, 'I miss you already, babe.' Alex didn't like the word 'babe'. It reminded her of the movie about the pig.

Alex thought she loved Kyle at some point. She'd heard rumours that he was going to break up with her, but she ignored them until one day he dumped her. She was so heartbroken that she didn't go out for four days. But she had to go to school. They hadn't spoken until today.

Alex went straight upstairs when she got in. She didn't enjoy her family's company. Her family was too loud, much louder than herself. Her brother and sister were constantly arguing. Her mum was trying to stop it, and then her baby sister was crying because of the noise. Alex was the eldest of them all, but was a lot quieter. The only place she could think was in her bedroom. She lay on her bed. She thought about Kyle. She thought about how they spent so much time together, about how much they loved each other and about their break-up. She continued to think about these things until she drifted to sleep.

Alex was still asleep when her mum came in and told her that there was someone at the door for her. She sat up and looked at the clock. It was half-past ten.

'Who would be knocking for me at this time?' she wondered aloud. She was surprised to see Kyle standing in the porch.

'You have to stop showing up unexpectedly.' She smiled faintly. He couldn't help smiling too. She was standing in her doorway, still in her uniform with her hair messed up.

'I love your just-awake look.' He laughed. She hit him lightly on the arm.

'Well I was asleep but then you decided to wake me up.' She tried to look as if she was angry but she couldn't keep a straight face.

'You're not an angry person, are you?'

'Not at all.' She looked into his eyes. She realised that his eyes weren't as dark as she'd thought. They were hazel. Kyle pulled Alex closer to him. She had her head buried in his chest but looked up. Their faces were so close that she could feel his breath on her cheeks. He kissed her. It wasn't like any of the kisses they had before. This one was different. This one was better. All of a sudden, she could feel herself fall for him all over again. When they had stopped after what felt like a million years, he pushed her away.

'I have something to tell you.' His voice was shaking.

She knew it was bad news. She breathed out heavily.

'I'm moving,' he said.

She stepped back.

'To where?'

'Boston. My mum got a new job.'

Alex couldn't speak. She could feel the tears welling up in her eyes.

'I'm sorry; I know I should have told you.'

'Yes! You should have!' Tears were starting to stream down her face now. 'You came here to tell me that you were moving, but instead you decide to kiss me and then tell me!' She was screaming now.

'I'm sorry, Alex. I really am.'

'When are you moving?'

He sighed. 'Two weeks.'

'I think you should go now, Kyle, I really do.' She didn't want to see him.

'But Alex—'

Alex cut him off. 'Just go!' She slammed the door in his face and ran upstairs. She had never cried so much. She buried her face into her pillow and cried some more. Eventually she fell asleep.

The next morning, she heard her mum come in but she ignored her. She didn't want to go to school. She didn't want to talk to anyone. She just wanted to be alone for now. She missed her trip to the cinema with Ciara. She was cut off from the world. A few days later Alex was just lying on her bed, fully dressed. She looked at the clock, it was almost four. She had forgotten that she dropped her phone the night Kyle had called, so she picked it up and turned it on. She had seventeen missed calls and twenty-two messages. Some of them were from Ciara but most of them were from Kyle. She didn't read them. She just deleted them all.

On Saturday, Orla knocked for her. Her mum let her upstairs. Alex was lying in bed with her laptop. Orla walked in, but Alex didn't hear her. Orla dived on her bed, landing on Alex's legs.

'Ow! That hurt! Get off me!' Orla was laughing.

She was still on Alex's legs when her brother walked in. 'Will you two stop shouting? I'm trying to do my homework!'

Alex pushed Orla off her bed.

He slammed the door.

'Why are you still in bed, Alex?' Orla asked, still laughing.

'Why not?' Alex replied.

'Do you really want to start this?' Orla always made her feel better. 'You're coming out with me tonight.'

'No, I'm not. I don't want to go out.' Alex buried her head in her pillow.

'You have no choice. You are coming out!'

'Fine. What are we doing?' Alex muffled from the pillow.

'Town. We're meeting a few of my friends in there.'

'Town? Do I have to?' Alex moaned.

'Yes! I have a friend that I think you'll like,' Orla winked.

'I don't want to meet another guy. We're not all like you,' Alex joked.

'Well then, Miss-I-Want-To-Stay-Single-For-The-Rest-Of-My-Life, I guess you won't get to meet Jake.'

'Jake?'

'No, Mary!' Orla said sarcastically.

'Oh…' Alex laughed. 'What time are we going at?'

'We're leaving at six.'

'Wow! You give me plenty of time to get ready, don't you?'

'Just hurry!'

Alex grabbed some jeans and a t-shirt and ran in to have a shower. It was almost five. She got out of the shower and Orla was lying on her bed with her laptop.

'Yes, you make yourself at home.' Alex laughed.

She was ready before six. They got on the bus.

'Where are we meeting your friends?'

'The Spire.'

They got off on O'Connell Street. There were crowds of tourists around the spire. A group of them waved at Orla. She grabbed Alex's arm and pulled her towards a guy. 'Alex, this is Jake.'

Jake was gorgeous, but he wasn't Kyle. She compared everyone to Kyle.

Over the next few months, she got set up with different guys, each one ending in disaster, just because none of them matched up to Kyle.

For Alex's seventeenth birthday, they went out for a meal, to the same place she went to with Kyle on their first date. For the whole night she was constantly thinking of him. She left early. Orla ran after her.

'What's wrong?' she asked.

Alex started running. She ran home. She wanted to go to Boston. She wanted to see Kyle. It had been nearly a year and she still couldn't forget about him. She was doing her Leaving Certificate in two months, so she was going to Boston straight after it.

She studied for two months straight; she didn't tell any of her friends about her plan.

She had everything ready. When Ciara and Orla found out they tried everything to stop her, but nothing could change her mind.

The week after her Leaving Cert ended, she boarded a plane to Boston. She spent the whole journey thinking of Kyle. She landed six hours later and got a taxi straight to his apartment. She rang the buzzer. His mum let her in. Kyle came down. He wasn't what he was a year ago. He wasn't the Kyle Alex knew. He was completely different. He wasn't what Alex wanted.

Alex realised that she had been waiting all this time for a sixteen-year-old Kyle and letting her dream of him stop her from moving on with her life. But he wasn't sixteen anymore. He wasn't Alex's Kyle. The dream was over. It was time to start living her life again.

Fresh Start
Shannon Granger

Ashley gets up early, sits on her bed and brushes her long brown hair. She looks for something to wear for her first day at college. She decides on skinny jeans and a funky t-shirt, with converse trainers and a leather jacket. She is looking forward to getting her hair and nails done, later on in the day, for her night out with the girls.

That evening, Ashley arrives home from college and gets ready for her night out. At half nine she arrives at the nightclub Pearls. All her friends are there and they are enjoying themselves a lot. She spots a nice-looking bloke. Ashley knows his face, but has never thought anything much of him until now. He is looking particularly well this evening.

Ashley carries on enjoying her night, but still has her eye on him. It looks as if he is checking her out too. Ashley goes outside on her own for some fresh air, because the place is so packed. There is no room to breathe. The bloke she has been watching follows her out. It looks as if he really wants to get talking to her.

'Are you having a good night?' he asks, walking over to her.

She smiles and says, 'Yes.'

They get chatting and she asks him his name.

'Stephen,' he tells her.

They exchange numbers. Ashley really likes him and it looks like he is into her too. She goes back into the club to her friends.

She tells her friends about him and they are all happy and smiley. But they also tell her to watch out. They know him, and know that all of his friends are wild. They have heard stories about them – stories about them taking drugs and being with different girls.

Stephen comes over to Ashley at the bar. 'Would you like to go for something to eat after this?' he asks. 'My mate is having a party in his penthouse. We could go back there later.'

Ashley's friends are planning on going home after the nightclub. They don't have a problem with her going home with the fella she has just met. They just warn her to be careful. Stephen is exactly Ashley's type. He is tall with a tight haircut, blue eyes and really white teeth. He is wearing nice trendy clothes too. He has a red Lyle and Scott t-shirt on, G-star jeans and Adidas black and red runners. Ashley thinks to herself, *he obviously looks after himself very well.*

They go to a nearby diner for something to eat, and then go back to Stephen's friend's house for the party.

Ashley gets a taxi home in the early hours of the morning. She has really enjoyed her night with Stephen and would like to see him again.

They text each other a lot, and he seems very into her. They end up getting together.

Ashley has her own home in San Francisco. She pays the rent and all the bills, as she works part-time for her dad's law firm. Everything is going great and she couldn't be any happier. Then Stephen moves in with Ashley.

Ashley is in college and training to be a lawyer. She only has six months left before she finishes her degree. Stephen is a male model for Calvin Klein, but hasn't got much work lately. He just lazes around the house, which Ashley isn't very happy with. Stephen and Ashley start to fight a lot, and he is becoming a control freak. He tries to tell her what to do. He is in her home doing nothing at all, just being a complete waster.

Ashley's friends don't want to know anything about him, because they don't like him one bit. He won't let her out with her friends or let her enjoy her life at all. She is losing her self-confidence because Stephen keeps putting her down. Ashley has not been with Stephen very long, and this has happened out of the blue. She is confused big time.

Ashley is having second thoughts about being with her boyfriend, but she carries on with him, and things begin to get worse and worse. One Saturday night she goes out to Pearls nightclub, where they first met. She looks very nice. She gets her hair and make-up done, and wears all new clothes. She meets up with her friends – she hasn't seen them in a long time. Stephen goes with her, of course! He doesn't bother telling Ashley she looks nice. He looks very unhappy when he sees people in the club looking at Ashley and telling her she is looking well.

The night moves on and Ashley is having a ball with all of her friends. At the end of the night she wants to go back to a party with them. There is no reason for her not to go. She is a young girl and has not got any kids.

'You're not going,' says Stephen firmly. He grabs the back of her little top, drags her out of the club and hits her. It is the first time he has ever hit her. It really hurts! Ashley gets a shock and starts crying. The nightclub they first met in is the same nightclub he first hits her in. She thinks it's very, very strange.

The next morning Ashley is still in shock. She has a black eye. She wonders why she is letting this happen to her. She really has to get away. She feels Stephen is a complete a psycho. It isn't like Ashley to think that about the love of her life. She has been blinded by love. Until that night, when he hit her.

Three days later she sits Stephen down and talks to him.

'I can't take this anymore. Get all of your stuff and get out of my life,' she tells him. She had wanted to say it straight away, but had to talk to her family and friends about what to say.

Stephen is shocked and can't believe what she has just said to him. He knows quite well he is in the wrong, but just won't admit it and say sorry. Ashley had let Stephen walk all over her, but not anymore. She is not going to let that shite happen again. It's over for good. No matter what he says to try and save himself, it's done!

One week later, Ashley is a new person. She is so glad that she stood her ground and stood up to Stephen. Why let someone treat you like that? she thinks. Why me? I have everything going for me. A beautiful family that I haven't seen in over two months because of him. I've the best friends anybody could ask for. Friends that I nearly lost because of Stephen. She realises that they were just worried about her and they wanted to look out for their close friend.

And soon, when she finishes college, she will have a great job. She would probably have failed her exams if she had stayed with Stephen, because of all the stress he put her under. He had tried to drag her down. But luckily she had copped on to what was good for her.

She is now able to go out with her friends, visit her family every second weekend in Las Vegas and do whatever she wants with nobody to answer to. She realises that she is much better off without him.

Ashley is quite happy with her life at the moment with Stephen not being in it. She barely sees him anymore and is happy, even though it's very hard sometimes and she misses him.

She finishes college and becomes a fully qualified lawyer. She buys a new sports car and moves into the city of San Francisco with one of her closest friends. Life is good.

In Love

Danielle Hand

Sasha was an 18-year-old girl in her last year at school. She was at home in bed asleep, when suddenly her alarm went off. She woke up and looked at her clock. It was 7.15 a.m.

Sasha jumped out of bed, went into the toilet, and washed herself. She then went back into her bedroom to get ready for school. She went downstairs when she was ready, and made tea and toast.

Sasha was a caring young girl who loved kids. She had a little brother called Joshua who was seven. She was expecting a little sister. She left her house after her breakfast and met her two best friends Alisha and Dominique at Castle Park in Swords. They all walked to school, chatting away and minding their own business.

Suddenly a group of boys walked into them. Sasha dropped her books and her friends helped her pick them up. They walked on and finally reached the school. Sasha felt embarrassed and a bit upset.

As soon as they began to walk into the gates, their principal said to them in a loud angry voice, 'YOU THREE ARE LATE.'

'Sorry sir,' said Sasha, in a sweet innocent voice. The three girls just walked on, and so did the principal.

In their first class all they did was chat about the school prom in two weeks' time. Their teacher knew they weren't listening, so she yelled at them saying, 'Since you three are too busy chatting about prom in my maths class, I will tell the principal that you are offering to do up the gym!'

The girls didn't want to do up the gym so they let out a little moan. They stayed quiet for the rest of the day and just listened in all of their classes, in case they got forced to help out with anything else in the school. A few hours passed and it reached four o'clock. It was time to go home.

Sasha walked home on her own because she knew Tom, Dominique's dad, collected Alisha and Dominique. Sasha got to the park and saw the same group of boys for the second time that day. She knew what was coming so she held her books tight, but they walked straight into her.

Her books fell once again. She bent down to pick them up and saw another hand on her history book. She followed that hand right up to the face. It was a young, handsome guy with dark spiked hair and a gorgeous smile. She looked at him for a few minutes then snapped out of it.

She said to him, 'Why are you helping me when it's your friends who keep on walking into me?'

He smiled and said, 'Don't mind those guys. They just think they're too cool.'

She smiled and said, 'It's okay.'

He helped her up and said, 'I'm Alex.'

She smiled at him and replied, 'I'm Sasha.'

They smiled at each other once more.

He asked her where she lived and she said, 'Oh, just ten minutes from here.'

He said, 'Come on, I live five minutes from you so I'll walk you.'

They walked and talked. Sasha laughed at his jokes even though they weren't funny. But she liked him a lot and she was sure he liked her too. When she got home she saw a note on her hall table.

It read: *Sorry, dear – I tried to call but your phone seems to be off. Anyways I'm gone to Grandma Kay's. Be home soon. Love, Mum.*

She put the note down and went up to her bedroom. She lay on her bed and did her homework. Then she called Alisha and Dominique and told them all about the cute guy she met in the park. They were raging that they hadn't seen him.

The next day she saw Alex again. He offered to walk her to school and Sasha just smiled.

Then Alex smiled too and said, 'I'll take that as a yes!'

They started to walk and chat away until they got near the park and saw all of Alex's friends. Alex saw them all and let out a little sigh. Sasha asked him what was wrong.

He replied, 'Oh nothing. Just hold your books tight.'

She knew what was up.

Alex hid his face and Sasha just looked at him and sighed. When Alex's friends got nearer they walked into her once again.

Alex rolled his eyes and said, 'Don't mind those dickheads!'

He helped her pick up all her books, and then he spotted a pink book. It wasn't a schoolbook – it had yellow writing on it saying *Sasha's diary: DO NOT TOUCH!!!* He picked it up and looked at the page it happened to open on. There were a lot of colourful butterflies on it and a big red heart with turquoise writing in it reading: *Sasha hearts Alex* ☺.

He smiled at her and handed her books to her. She noticed the smile on his face and said to him, 'What are you smiling at?' She gave a little giggle. He wouldn't answer her – just kept on smiling. They walked on, chatting about school.

Sasha thought Alex was a very nice guy and asked him, 'Why do you bother with the group of boys who walked into me?'

Alex was quiet for a minute and then he said to her, 'I don't exactly know, to be honest; I guess they're all I have!'

She looked at him. They finally got to the gates where she met Alisha and Dominique. They called her, so she told Alex that she would catch him later. Sasha then went over to her friends and they all walked to class.

When it reached four o'clock the bell went. They all walked home together. When Sasha got to her house she said hello to her mum and brother. She then went up to her bedroom and logged onto Facebook. She had one friend request and it was from Alex, so she accepted him. She then got a message from him saying: *Hey, didn't see you after school today, how come? Anyway, are you free Thursday night?*

Sasha sat there looking at the computer screen thinking, what will I say? Will I even write back? She didn't know what to do. She felt really excited and scarlet at the same time. After about five minutes she replied: *Hey. Oh I walked home with Alisha and Dominique today. Oh, about tomorrow night – yes, I am.* She signed out and rang her friends to tell them all about Alex adding her and texting her and asking her to go on a date with him. She told them she decided to go and she couldn't wait. They knew she liked him and they were delighted for her.

The next day came. It was Wednesday. She met her friends in the park again. She then saw Alex and went really red in the face. She was so embarrassed. He called her and ran over to her. She stood there, still red. He looked at her and smiled.

Dominique and Alisha looked at the two of them and said, 'Eh, we're just going to go into the hall to choose ideas for the prom, so we'll see you in there, OK?'

Sasha just said, 'Yeah, sure, I'll follow you in.'

Alex asked her if she was still up for the following night. She said, 'Oh yeah, of course. Where are we going?'

He smiled at her and said, 'Cool, and it's a surprise.' He winked at her.

She started to laugh and said, 'Oh, OK.'

They both walked into the school and he walked her to the hall. She thanked him and went over to join her friends.

On Friday she went to school all excited. She couldn't wait until that night. She went to the hall to see Alisha and Dominique. They were silent for a while and to break the silence Alisha asked Sasha: 'What are you wearing on your date tonight?'

Sasha replied, 'I don't know yet. I don't even know where he's taking me.'

Later that day she went home and had her dinner. She started to get ready at 6.45 p.m. It would take ages to do her hair, so she did that first. By the time she got around to getting dressed it was 7.45 p.m. When she was ready, Alex knocked at her door. Her mum, Laura answered it. She told him to come in, so he did.

They left by nine o'clock. He took her to a fancy restaurant in the city called Nico's. The food was gorgeous and expensive, but Alex paid for it all. He then took her to a ballet in the Liberty Theatre. She loved it. Alex looked at Sasha and there was a teardrop rolling down her cheek. He asked her what was wrong. She told him that she used to be in ballet until she was fifteen.

Alex asked her why had she left it and she looked at him. She knew she could trust him, so she said to him, 'I started ballet when I was eight and left when I was fifteen because of something that happened my dad. He was the only one that could boost my confidence up, the only one I believed in. I wouldn't do any competitions or plays unless my dad was at them. My big day came and my dad said to me, "I will be there, don't worry. I promise I won't let you down." I believed him. When the bus came I was ready and my dad said to me, "Go win that Trophy!" and then he kissed me on the cheek and gave me one of his famous bear hugs. We arrived at the theatre in Sligo and started warming up. I was on second and when I walked onto the stage I looked round but couldn't see my dad. I asked them if I could call my mum before I started. One of the judges said, "Yes, sure, no problem," so I did. When she answered I said to her, "Mam, where's Dad? He isn't here; he told me he would be here." My mum told me to calm down and that he would be there. I calmed down.

'My mum then said, "He will be there, don't worry." I hung up and went back out to the stage.' Alex looked at her as they were walking out of Liberty Hall Theatre.

He said to her, 'Sasha, you don't have to tell me if it's going to upset you.'

She said to him, 'I want to tell you, but…'

He took her by the hand and said, 'OK.' Sasha continued: 'Anyway, I started my dance because I wanted to win so bad. I danced for ten minutes and when I finished my dad was still nowhere to be found. At this point I was just so angry I wanted to kill my dad.'

Alex smiled and said, 'I know that feeling.' But he looked at her again and stopped. Sasha continued, 'Anyway, when we all finished I got named as first-place winner. I was so happy but still angry with my dad. When I got home I opened the door, and was met by my mum. There were two cops in the living room. My mum was crying. I asked the girl cop what was wrong and she said to me, "I think you should sit down for this, sweetheart." I had a feeling that this was bad, so I sat down and the news just hit me. The cop said to me, "Your father has been in a car crash on his way to your show. I am very sorry but he did not survive.'"

As Sasha was telling Alex this, she started to sob. He took her by both hands and gave her a hug. He was asking her was she OK and she said yes. She took his hand and they both walked to the car. It was cold and late, but she didn't mind, because she was with Alex. When they got back they sat on her mum's swing chair in the garden and chatted. Anytime Alex looked at her she could feel her heart melt. They looked into each other's eyes and suddenly Alex leaned in to kiss her. They kissed a bit and then her mum came out. Sasha gave Alex a kiss goodnight and went in.

Alex drove home chuffed that he was with Sasha now. He couldn't wait to see her tomorrow.

Sasha went to bed smiling. She was very happy that Alex was now her boyfriend, but still sad about her dad.

The next day she told her friends everything. She got a message on her phone from Alex saying 'Are you in school?'

She replied: 'Yes. Where are you?'

They met each other at the gate and his friend Jason was with him. Jason liked Dominique. They'd been on a date and it hadn't worked out, but they thought they would give it another chance tonight.

Friday night came and it was prom night! They were all doing the hall up for it and couldn't wait until later. At 8 o'clock they were all in Alisha's house waiting on the limo. It came at 8.15 p.m. They got into it headed to the prom. There were three couples in the limo: Alisha and Derek, Sasha and Alex, and Dominique and Jason. They all arrived at the prom. They got pictures taken and they danced. The prom was brilliant. It was designed very well. The DJ set was on the stage and behind the set there was a huge sign on the wall. It was very colourful, and read: 'Welcome to a Night of Dreams'. The walls were covered in pink and white balloons, there was lots of confetti on the ground, and a big huge silver disco ball was shining everywhere. There was a white net with red balloons on each corner of the ceiling. There were girls in really long silk dresses in various colours and the guys were all in black tuxedos with different coloured ties.

Sasha found Alex in the crowd and gave him a hug and a kiss and apologised for the night before. That ballet was just too much for her, especially when it was her dad's anniversary. That was why she had been so upset, she explained quietly.

Alex said, 'Oh, I'm so sorry, you should have told me.'

'Oh it's fine.' She said.

Alex said to her, 'Don't worry, I'm always here for you, no matter what.'

She smiled.

When they stopped talking Sasha heard her favourite song, which was Aerosmith's 'Don't Wanna Miss a Thing', which was also her father's funeral song. She asked Alex to dance, so they did. They danced, laughed, got in pictures and danced some more. They had the best time of their lives. The prom really took Sasha's mind off her dad for a while. Alex was dancing with her to the last song and he kissed her and said, 'Sasha, I know we have just started going out, but I know for a fact that I already love you.'

Sasha felt a flicker of happiness. She had never expected to feel happy again, but in her new boyfriend's arms she knew she was making a fresh start.

Le CHEAT
Eoghan Higgins

Here we were, my dad and I, in Paris for the second leg of the World Cup play-off against France. The first leg had been in Croke Park and, to the disappointment of my friends and I – and a lot of Irish supporters – we were 1–0 down to a Nicolas Anelka goal.

The scene was set for a gripping ninety minutes of football, or so we thought! The grass was freshly cut and watered and plenty of Irish fans had travelled to the match as we had done. The French team were ready to fight for a place in South Africa and Trapattoni's men were ready to give them a hard time. The Irish fans were singing 'The Fields of Athenry' as the two sides warmed up. It was a wonderful sight to see, with the Irish minority making most of the noise in the stadium.

All started well and our team were defending well against a strong French attack, whose players included Thierry Henry, Nicolas Anelka, Yohann Gourcuff and Marseille's new €10-million euro signing André-Pierre Gignac. Lucky for our team, star player Franck Ribéry was missing through injury.

The game was going fantastic from an Irish point of view, with our team trying to make the most of our chances. With about fifteen minutes left until half-time we scored! A blistering goal from Irish hero Robbie Keane: the fans went wild. It was such a beautiful play as well and not just another trademark scrappy goal. A fantastic chip-through ball from Kilbane to Duff, who succeeded to keep the ball in play with a lovely pass back into the box to find Keane, who coolly slid the ball into the bottom right-hand corner of the French net. My dad and I were extremely happy with the goal and there was a sense of real ecstasy from the away fans and the away team too. A well-deserved goal to put us level on aggregate goals going into half-time.

France started the second half better, with fewer passes going astray. Ireland also started well, but you could tell the Irish were starting to tire. Yet we managed to hold on. France had their chances, as did we, but no goals could be put in the net.

Both teams were attacking with real flair and we thought we had a goal when the ball landed to Glenn Whelan inside the area. But the French goalkeeper Lloris produced yet another good save. We were all hoping for another chance at goal to arise, but we were not sure if one would.

The teams edged closer to extra time and were level, with little sign of a goal to come from either side. The referee blew his whistle, indicating that the ninety minutes were up and it would in fact take extra time and maybe even penalties to separate the two teams. There were mixed reactions going into extra time, some wondering if the Irish had the legs to carry on for another thirty minutes, while others thought penalties were most certainly on the cards.

It was about halfway through the first half of extra time and both teams were looking quite tired. France was awarded a free kick on the halfway line. The ball was kicked up the pitch with force; nobody seemed to have headed it out. It was going out of play, surely, but for a Thierry Henry handball which kept the ball in play. Henry kicked the ball across the Irish goal for William Gallas to head the ball in the back of the net from close range – but surely the officials saw the hand. They did not. The goal was allowed; we felt sick. The Irish were shouting.

'The ref's blind!'

'Henry's a cheater!'

The Irish knew Henry had used his hand; Henry knew he had used his hand and we were starting to think the French fans knew it as well. The match ended 1–1 and 2–1 on aggregate to France. Ireland was not going to be one of the thirty-two teams competing in the 2010 World Cup in South Africa because of a blatant handball.

The FAI tried to get a replay, but FIFA refused and the Ireland team and fans did not travel to South Africa. The French team came last in their group, the manager was fired and several players were suspended.

Ireland's summer wasn't *all* bad.

The Dressing Room
Alan Keegan

It was eleven o'clock and Brian and Niall were walking in from their small break. They were in Science class talking about a big Gaelic match they had in a few days. Brian and Niall were the two best players on the team and they were great friends. The class were on their way down to PE and they were the first two down in the hall. Both of them had changed before the rest of the class got there. They started messing around in the hall for a while. A few minutes later the class came in and the teacher made them all warm up and do a few laps of the hall. After that the teacher let them play football until the class was over.

They went into the dressing room with the others to get changed. Brian went into the toilet and Niall took out his drink. He spilled a drop on the floor by accident and he didn't clean it up. Brian walked out of the toilet and nobody told him that the floor was wet. He slipped on Niall's spilt drink and fell on his side. A few people started laughing because they didn't know he was really hurt. Niall stopped laughing when he realised it was serious and asked Brian if he was okay. The teacher helped Brian up and brought him to the nurse's office and she gave him some ice and a bandage.

After school Brian went to the hospital to get an x-ray on his arm. He was sitting in the waiting room for a while, waiting on the results. Eventually the doctor came back. He told Brian that he had broken his elbow and would need an operation on it. Brian was

angry because he had to play in a match for the school the following week and now he wouldn't be able to.

He had to get a cast on his arm and he would have to wear it for a few weeks, the doctor explained. Brian went in to hospital and had the operation. He wasn't in school the day after it because his elbow hurt him too much.

The following Monday Brian came into school. Niall avoided him all day. Brian didn't realise that the water on the floor was from Niall's drink, so Brian wasn't angry with him. Brian asked Niall who threw the water on the floor and Niall looked a bit embarrassed and said that he didn't know. Brian asked a few other people out of the class and they all said that they didn't know and they hadn't seen anybody pouring it on the floor. Brian was angry with the whole class because nobody would tell him who had done it. The Gaelic teacher asked him what had happened. Brian told him. The

Gaelic teacher asked him who had spilt the water and Brian said:

'Nobody knows.'

The teacher was worried that they would lose the match because one of their best players wasn't going to be able to play. The Gaelic manager asked Niall in front of Brian if he would like to be the Captain. Niall said, 'Yes.' Brian's face went red with anger because he had lost the captaincy of the team.

Later, Brian and Niall were walking home to Brian's house. When they got there Niall told Brian about spilling the water from his drink in the dressing room. Brian was speechless. Then he started to shout at Niall:

'Why didn't you tell me that the water was there before I walked on it?'

Niall told him that he'd forgotten, that he hadn't though that he'd walk on it. Brian told Niall to get out of his house. Brian didn't go to school the next day because he was so pissed off about Niall breaking his elbow.

It was the day of the match. Brian had seen the team going to the grounds on the bus on his way to school and he decided to go and watch the match with some other friends. The game started and Niall got the first point. At half-time the match was evenly scored. At the start of the second half, Niall got another few points and put his team in the lead. The match was nearly over and Niall got into a bad tackle and had to come off for the rest of the game. Niall's team won and they were all celebrating.

The next day in school Brian bumped into Niall and ignored him, acting like he wasn't even there. Niall kept trying to apologise, but Brian just kept ignoring him and acted as if he didn't exist. A few weeks after the match, when Brian got his cast off, he was playing Gaelic again and got back the captaincy. When the teacher and the principal found out that Niall had spilt the water on the floor, Niall got suspended from school for two weeks.

But Brian got over his anger with Niall because they had been friends for a long time. Niall came back from suspension and was walking down the hall on his own when Brian saw him. He went over and started talking to his friend and they were back to normal and not fighting anymore. Life was too short to hold a grudge.

Rotten Centre

Damien McKevitt

This story begins in a rundown old town in the middle of an island. The town is called Rotten Centre. In the middle of this town there is a little bit of land. In the middle of the little bit of land there is a building that was once the mayor's home.

Grey sand stretches as far as the eye can see. People live in Rotten Centre, but they look different to everyone else who lives around the coast of this wasteland. The buildings have been weather-worn over the years and have been abandoned, as most of the families died from breathing in too much sand. The sand caused their lungs to shrink, which made it difficult for them to breathe. This was followed by death.

The weather in this town is the same most of the time. It rains a lot. If it is not raining, it is cold. Not long ago there was a storm that went on for so long that a lake appeared after it. It was a strange lake, like a moat around the town. The lake did not help the people that lived there. Six people died because of it. The dead included the mayor of the town and a family of five. The people of the town that had been surrounded by the lake began to create a bridge so the food suppliers could deliver food to the other towns more rapidly. In the middle of the town is a district known as Latin's Home. Latin's Home is at the very centre of Rotten Centre. It is a very small area with only a small number of inhabitants. No one else has set foot in the place for years. People think it is a weird name. But it isn't. Years

ago Latins found this little island and moved to the centre of the island so they would be safe from invaders. They remained safe for over a thousand years until the British invaded and took over the island.

Most of the history books are written in Latin, but nobody can speak Latin these days, so the history of the island has been lost. Now, in 1849, a family of five lives in the mayor's old home. The building has been improved, as it is over one hundred years old.

The five members of the family are Ashley (aged 16), Mary (aged 21), Patrick (aged 22), Carlos (aged 7) and Lisa (aged 3). Carlos was adopted into the family at the age of two, when his own family moved away to somewhere in Germany. Carlos was left on a doorstep. Luckily a woman found him on the doorstep that evening and brought him in to her home. The temperature dropped to minus ten that night. Had she not found Carlos there, he would have frozen to death.

He soon became accepted as part of the family and was happy with them. The years sped by.

Mary and Patrick have become like parents to Carlos since their own parents died in an accident not that long ago. A lot of people say they just upped and left, but the family does not believe that they would have left them behind like that. There are lots of stories about what might have happened them, too many to recount here. Despite the variety of stories, they all end with a note, written in Latin and left behind by the father. Nobody knows what it means.

In the middle of winter there is a snowstorm so bad that the schools close. With no school to go to, Ashley sits at home, wondering why no one in his family knows Latin. He thinks about the letter and asks his older brother Patrick for the note, as he has it in his room. That afternoon Ashley walks past his school, which is just around the

corner from his house. He glimpses a book from the corner of his eye, lying in the gutter. He picks it up to find it is an old, tattered Latin dictionary. The pages are wet and stuck together. Ashley goes home quickly and asks for the note that Patrick found the night of his parents' disappearance. Patrick had found the note outside their home before hearing about his parents. Ashley spots the note and asks Patrick can he have it. He wants to use the dictionary to help him understand the note.

Patrick says, 'No. Why would I give it to you?'

Ashley replies, showing the Latin dictionary to Patrick. 'I may be able to use this to help me.'

Patrick sits there in shock and says, 'OK, here you go.'

Ashley thanks his brother, with a big smile on his face.

Ashley is disappointed when it turns out that he cannot make out any of the words, even with help from the dictionary. Ashley is puzzled.

The next morning he goes to the big building in the centre of the town square. This building has Latin words written all over it and there are statues all along the outside of this building. He looks at them, but none of them are the same as the words as on the note. That afternoon he goes around town asking people if they know any Latin words at all. It looks like no one can help him. But then one elderly man stops. He says he knows some Latin and will help him. The elderly man is very well dressed and he looks very innocent. Ashley asks him what his name is and how long he has been living there.

'I have lived here for all of my fifty-one years,' he says. 'I know your face from somewhere.'

'Well I don't remember ever seeing you before.'

The old man says, 'What is your name son? Is it Ashley?'

'Yeah. How do you know my name?' Ashley is surprised.

The elderly man tells him, 'Because I am your grandfather.'

Ashley could not remember ever meeting his grandfather. He disappeared shortly after Ashley's parents left, and Ashley had not seen him for a long time before that. Patrick and Mary had always thought he was dead, as they heard people talking about an old man who had hanged himself in the local park.

Ashley is shocked. He has just found his grandfather whom he hasn't seen since his eighth birthday. Ashley asks him what the note says. His grandfather writes down in Latin:

Nos es rumex super subitus recedentia; nos operor ignoro si vel ut nos mos redeo. They evestigatus nostrum specialis quod is est pro vestri own bonus ut vos don't expiscor, vestri sincerely, vestri loving parentes.

He then tells Ashley what it means in English:

We are sorry about sudden disappearance; we do not know if or when we will come back. They found out our secret and it is for your own good that you don't find out, yours sincerely, your loving parents.

Ashley's grandfather tells him that the secret might be in the building with the statues around the outside of it. He also tells him to be very careful where he goes and what he does. The grandfather stays the night in their house and tells him how to prepare for entry into the building. It is not something that can be done quickly.

Ashley wakes up early the next morning. Just as he is about to walk out the door, his grandfather grabs him and says, 'Where do you think you are going?'

'I am going out to my mate's house.'

His grandfather is angry. 'Don't lie to me. You are going to the building.'

Before Ashley has a chance to answer, his grandfather says, 'Don't be in such a hurry. Maybe I was wrong. It's nothing special.'

Mary comes home from work that afternoon. She had to work through the night so she wasn't home the previous day. She starts to prepare dinner and then notices her grandfather. She freezes for a few seconds and jumps, filled with happiness, as she has not seen him for years.

After they have their dinner, Ashley says he is going to his friend's house. Instead, he runs to the building. When he gets to the building he takes a deep breath and goes in. He looks around. He cannot see anything but a light coming from the floorboards. He opens the door and, as he enters the building, the door slams behind him. So he walks into the darkness, blind to his surroundings, not knowing what is around him. He makes his way around by touch, as it is so dark. As he turns around the corner, he sees a torch shining on a wall that is covered in blood. On the floor in front of him is a body, with nothing but bone remaining. He runs as fast as he can to get away from the horrible smell of rotting flesh coming from that room. There is a second body just behind him. He makes his way to a door. He opens it, enters, and closes it behind him. Ashley looks around and finds a picture of a baby, with its parents holding it, smiling. He looks closer and sees that it looks just like his parents. He wipes the bottom of the frame, revealing his own name, *ASHLEY TOMPSON*, in thick, dark bold red writing. He hears a loud noise and runs to the next room to see a staircase that leads down to a very bright light. He makes his way towards it, not knowing what is ahead of him. A loud scream shakes his eardrums. He puts his hands over his ears, but it doesn't make a difference. He makes his way up the stairs and past the picture of himself. Past the room full of blood. And finally out the front door to see the light of day. He finds it strange that it is daytime, as it was night when he went in. Finally he makes it to his front door, still in shock.

The next morning Patrick asks if he was really in his mate's house.

'Of course,' Ashley says.

Patrick doesn't think he is telling the truth and asks his grandfather, 'Where was Ashley last night?'

His grandfather tells him everything. Patrick decides that he has to go to the building himself, despite his grandfather's warnings about it. He goes in at the crack of dawn. He enters the building. He is able to see, as it is bright. He takes a totally different route to Ashley's. He ends up in an old chamber that looks as if it could still be used. He looks around for signs. He sees a brightly coloured treasure chest.

So it *is* true then: the rumours that he had heard when he was a boy. There is treasure that may contain powers to change the course of history if it ends up in the wrong hands. Patrick doesn't have the key to the chest. He tries to open it, pulling and pushing, but it will not move. He grows tired from trying to open it. 'If only I had the key,' he thinks. He does not know that now he has touched the chest he will never leave the building ever again.

Two days pass. All the family are very worried about Patrick. The grandfather calls the local police station. The police go to the building and search for hours. They go up to the very top of the building and then down to the basement. They find three bodies. Ashley thinks that one of them could be Patrick. The police won't tell them what they saw, and it is too disturbing even to write it in a report.

After his brother's horrible death, Ashley leaves to go to the southern part of the island with the rest of his family. Ten years later Ashley gets married. His sister also gets married. Ashley and his wife have two boys and Mary has a girl and a boy. The year Ashley has his second boy, policemen carry out a huge investigation of the strange building. But nothing is revealed.

Two years go by after Ashley and Mary and the rest of the family move away. Carlos decides to go back. He goes into the building and he hears screams. It is like his brother and parents are calling for him.

Carlos writes a book about what happened to his parents and brother. He sells millions of copies of his book worldwide. He makes a great living. He makes it seem as if something was trying to kill his parents and brother. It appears as though spirits of some sort killed them, as there was no evidence found at the scene. The only other explanation put forward was that they all killed each other in a fit of madness, but there was no weapon or fingerprints found.

Ashley decided to put the past behind him. He got a good job and made lots of money to look after his family. Ashley died at the age of seventy-seven. His sons are still alive today. Carlos and his son and daughter are still living off the millions that Carlos made from the books he wrote. They all live a life of luxury.

Carlos discovered that their grandfather was a spirit, trying to get Ashley to go to find the chest and tell him where it was so that the grandfather could have the power to do whatever he wanted.

Maybe he would have brought himself back to life to take over the world, or he might have had good intentions and intended to save the world from poverty, doomsday or even save the planet from the apocalypse. Nobody will ever know. His plan didn't work and he never got the chance to see the chest. Patrick lost his life because of him, but Ashley and Carlos escaped the same fate and survived to tell the strange tale.

My Friends and Me

Tomás Nguyen

My name is Anthony and I live in an apartment block in Coolock. My best friends are Craig, Stephen and Michael. We drive around in my car, cruising. I work for a Chinese company, doing deliveries. Craig, Stephen and Michael always buzz around with me in the car. We always have a laugh, and when I'm off we buzz out drinking, the lot of us. My mate Craig has a girlfriend, Jenny. They are getting married in two weeks. Michael will be moving to Cavan soon.

We have a plan that the day before he goes we're going to throw a party for him and we're going to go to a club. In two months, the lot of us are planning on going to Ibiza for Stephen's birthday. He's going to be twenty-one. He's going to apply for his licence for the car. He keeps telling us that he's going to get a Toyota Glanza, but his insurance would be very dear. I tell him that he should start off with a smaller car. Once he gets that all sorted he won't be getting in my car – ha! He also talks to me about getting a job. He wants to be a mechanic, fixing cars. His dad used to be a mechanic. Stephen always told us, when he was younger, that he wanted to be just like his dad.

My plans are to go back to school and go to college. I was kicked out in sixth year for being an eejit. I'm glad I'm going back because I'm planning on getting a job in a factory. So I'm going to get the Leaving Cert and go straight to college to do a course in safety regulations for factories.

It's Friday and now we're all talking about Craig's big day. I'd say it will be a buzz! The lot of us are going. I'm going to be best man. Can't wait.

'Aw, Anthony,' Craig says to me. 'I'm buzzing up to the bank to withdraw a few bob. Ya buzzing up, man?'

'I can't, man. Busy today. Have to sort a few things out, ya know.'

'Alrigh',' says Craig. 'No prob, man. Be back in a few.'

I walk off and leave him to it.

So I'm just sitting back on the couch when the six o'clock news comes on. I'm watching it and it says there's a man in hospital with stab wounds. The name of this young man is Craig Connell. As soon as I hear this I'm snapping. I go up to the hospital to see him. Jenny is there, sobbing. I ask her if I can have a word with Craig. Jenny walks out and I start talking to Craig. I ask him was if he's all right and all. So we're talking about what happened, and I ask him, 'Who did it?'

He just tells me all he remembers is getting into his car and a gang approaching him, giving out loads. Then, before he knew it, the money that he had withdrawn from the bank for the wedding was gone and he was on the ground in pain, because he had been stabbed.

So I say to him, 'I'm going to find these eejits that did this to you. I swear I will.'

'You're only going to get yourself in trouble, Anthony,' says Craig.

I walk out of the room pissed off about what happened Craig. I hop into my car and drive around looking for the gang that did this to my friend. I don't see anyone. But one of my mates, Ger, tells me that he thinks he knows who robbed Craig. I drive around a bit more but don't find them. But I plan to go out again the next day and the day after until I do.

I'm driving around again. I see a bunch of young fellas in a car in a laneway. I get out of mine and walk over to them. They're in the car counting money. One of them hops out and I say to him, 'Here, where did ya get that money, man?'

The chap says, 'Never mind where I got it. It has nothing to do with you, all right?'

I say, 'All right,' and walk back to the car. But the gang starts following me. They threaten me. I know who they are. They tell me not to say anything. I'm getting angry. One of them pushes me. I'm really angry now.

I take out a gun. I've had a gun for a long time but I've never used it. I step back. I start shooting the people that did this to my friend Craig. Now I'm scared. What have I done? I run straight to the car, get in, turn the ignition and take off. I'm driving around. I'm shaking. I want to go to the hospital to see Craig.

I'm nearly there, but there's a garda checkpoint. The garda says, 'Sorry, you wouldn't just pull over to the side of the road there, would ya?'

I'm frightened but I pull over. The guards start searching me and I tell them, 'Here, officer. I've nothing on me. Will ya let me go?'

The garda says, 'You in a rush or something?'

I say, 'Yeah, I am, guard. I'm goin' to see a friend in the hospital.'

The garda says, 'Do you mind if I search the car?'

I do mind. I don't want them to search the car, but I say, 'Sure. Go ahead. I have nothing to hide.'

So the garda begins to search the car. The gun is under the driver's seat. The garda is still searching and looks under the driver's seat. He says, 'What's this here, sonny?'

I say, 'I don't know where that has come from.'

The garda says, 'Sure, sure. I would like some details.'

'Me name is Anthony. I'm from Coolock. I live in an apartment. I live down past

Clonshaugh. Coolock apartments,' I tell the garda.

'All right, Anthony. I'm arresting you for possession of a gun. You don't have to say or do anything, but if you do say or do anything it may be used as evidence later in court,' says the garda.

So I'm arrested. The garda tells me I can phone someone, but I don't. I'm going to be in court the next day. They take my phone.

I'm sure everyone's trying to ring me to talk about Craig. They haven't got a clue where I am or what's happened. I don't know if anyone I know will be in court.

They're driving me there and as we go past the snooker hall I see everyone standing outside. Craig is there. His arm is in a sling. He doesn't look well. I don't think he should be out of the hospital. The lads are having a smoke. I ask the garda to stop so as I can say hello to my mates. They let me out of the car.

I shout at Craig, 'Sorry, pal. I've been arrested. I don't think I can be your best man.'

I walk towards Craig. And then I run. I do a legger on the gardaí. They start chasing me.

I make it to my pal Michael's house. I ask him to let me stay there for a while. At first he doesn't want to. Then he says OK. But not for long.

Now it's Wednesday. I've arranged a flight to England. I'm doing a runner on the gardaí. I don't want to go to prison. I'm up early for my flight. I'm all dressed up, and I say good luck and bye to Michael. I hop in the taxi.

The taxi driver is talking and I'm talking back and he goes, 'So where are you going, Anthony?'

I jump around, a bit shocked that he knows my name, but I play it cool. 'To the airport please. And how do you know my name, anyways?'

The taxi man goes, 'You're that fella who shot my son, aren't you?'

I'm really shocked now. I don't know him, but he knows me.

'No ... Why?' I say.

I start panicking, and think *who's this*?

'You bleeding are,' shouts the taxi driver. 'You shot him in cold blood, you bastard.'

'I swear it wasn't me. Just drop me to the airport, will ya?'

I'm a little aggressive now. I just want to get away.

So we're nearly at the airport. The taxi driver pulls into a lane and I try to get out of the car. The taxi man pulls out a gun. I'm shocked. Where did that come from? What's happened? I feel a bit dizzy. I'm in pain. I feel my chest throbbing, and there is something wet rolling down my head. Then the taxi man just dumps me out of the car, jumps back in and drives off. I see a man walking down the lane. He's looking at me lying on the ground, covered in blood. I hear him. I say to him, 'I'm afraid of dying.'

The man walks over to a phone box and rings the ambulance and the gardaí. So the gardaí are there investigating what happened. They ask the man did he see what happened. The man says, 'No. I was just walking my dog and I saw this man lying here.'

Then I'm rushed to hospital and my friends haven't got a clue where I am except Michael! But then the news gets out and they all arrive and are around the bed with me and I can hear them. They're all thinking, 'I hope he stays alive.' I think it's mad that I can hear them thinking in their heads. None of their mouths are moving.

A nurse comes in. She looks like she has something to tell them. 'He was shot seven times. Six times in the upper body area and once in the head. We could not save him.'

All the lads start crying and saying, 'Why? Why Anthony? He was like a brother to us. Why?'

Then a priest comes in to give me the last rites.

I know I'm dead.

Love Story
Karen Nolan

Ashley was a quiet girl and didn't like trouble. She had long brown hair and was tall and skinny. She was looking for her first real job and was very nervous, so nervous that she didn't know what to wear. She tried on everything she owned, but she just couldn't make her mind up. She didn't know what looked the best on her. Finally she decided on her good black trousers, her white and black blouse and her new black leather coat with black glitter shoes.

She printed her CVs out and headed to town to hand them into shops. She thought about where she would hand them out and what kind of job she would like to do. She had always loved cooking, so she decided to hand some CVs in to restaurants to see what would happen. Ashley was walking through town looking at all the different restaurants and one caught her eye. It was lovely. From the outside it looked pretty and buzzy. Ashley went in and there were lots of people sitting down eating and chatting away.

Ashley was in a daze looking at the restaurant and how lovely it was. She walked into a waiter and all of her CVs fell to the floor. Ashley was so embarrassed that she ran straight in to the toilets. When she came out again the waiter was standing there with her CVs. She just looked at him. She was too embarrassed to even say thank you. The waiter handed her the CVs and said, 'Are you OK?'

Ashley just looked at him. 'Yes,' she said. 'I'm grand. Thanks for picking up the CVs.'

'You're welcome,' he said.

Ashley managed to pull herself together and asked the waiter could she leave a CV with him to give to the manager. She was stammering with nerves.

He smiled at her. 'I will, of course,' he said. 'By the way, I'm Paul. What's your name?'

'I'm Ashley.'

'That's a lovely name,' Paul replied. 'I will give your CV to the boss. Good luck.'

'Thank you,' said Ashley.

As she walked out of the restaurant she felt as if everyone was looking at her. She started to laugh when she got outside. It had been really embarrassing, but at least she'd left her CV there.

Ashley continued walking around town handing out CVs. She was a bit more confident now. By half eight she was getting tired of walking around. It was freezing out. She decided to go get the bus home. As she was waiting on the bus, she saw someone walking towards her. It was the waiter from the restaurant. She turned her head, hoping that he wouldn't notice her. All of a sudden, she felt someone tipping her arm. She turned around and it was him, Paul. He looked at Ashley and said, 'Hello.' Ashley was so embarrassed she could feel her face going red.

Paul said, 'I handed your CV in. The boss was impressed with it, so I'd say you'll be getting a phone call soon.'

'Well thanks for giving it to him,' Ashley replied. 'I hope I get the job.'

Ashley and Paul started to chat. They were chatting so much that the bus drove past.

'What am I going to do?' said Ashley. 'There isn't another bus for ages and I don't have money for a taxi.'

Paul just laughed.

'It's not funny. What am I going to do?'

'Come with me,' said Paul.

Ashley didn't know what to do. She went with him.

'Where are you bringing me?' she asked.

'Wait and see.'

Ashley didn't know where she was going. Then she saw a car.

'Hop in,' said Paul, smiling.

Ashley just looked at him.

'I'm not going to bite you,' he said. 'You need a lift, so get in!'

Ashley smiled and hopped into the car.

'So where do you live?' Paul asked.

'Swords.'

She hoped he wouldn't mind driving all the way to Swords. He just nodded and started up the car.

So Ashley and Paul started to talk again. They talked and talked and she suddenly realised that he was driving past the turn to her house.

'You've just missed my turn!' she cried.

'Don't worry. I'll turn back around.'

At last they were outside Ashley's home.

'That's a nice house,' said Paul.

'Yeah. It's my mam and dad's house.

When I get a job I might be able to get a place of my own.'

After a moment's silence, Ashley said, 'Well, I'd better go.'

'No problem,' Paul said. 'I hope you get the job. I'll put a word in for you.'

Ashley looked at him and smiled. As she was getting out, Paul grabbed her and looked at her. Then he kissed her. She didn't know what to do.

He smiled at her and said, 'Here's my number. When you're free call me.'

'Yes. I'd love to!' Ashley said getting out of the car.

Paul drove away. Ashley was so happy she couldn't stop smiling. All she wanted to do was call him. But she didn't want him to think she was an easy girl to get.

The next day Ashley got a phone call from the boss in the restaurant asking her to come in for an interview. She was delighted. She didn't know what to wear again. She went into her room and rooted for something. She had nothing nice so she went into her sister's room and looked in her wardrobe. She borrowed a blue skirt and top and went back into her room to get ready.

Her dad came into her. 'Where you off to?' he said.

'I have an interview in a restaurant in town.'

'Do you want a lift?'

'Yes, if you wouldn't mind, Dad. I'll be down in a minute.'

Ashley's dad dropped her off and wished her luck. She walked in, went over to one of the waiters and asked where the boss was. The waiter brought her down to him. She was very nervous again but she got through the interview and then he told her she got the job. She didn't know what to say, she was so happy. As she was walking out of the boss's office she saw Paul. He came over to her and asked how she got on.

'I got the job!' said Ashley.

He gave her a hug. 'That kiss last night was great.'

'I enjoyed it too.'

'Well, I gotta go,' he said.

'I guess I'll see you at work.'

'You will,' said Paul.

Later, as Ashley was walking to the bus stop, she saw Paul and another girl. They were talking and then he kissed her on the cheek. She felt sick to her stomach. The bus came and she hopped on it. The next day she got up for work. She didn't want to go. She didn't want to see Paul. She just felt sick. She got into work ten minutes early so she could get her uniform.

Paul came in after her.

'I saw you yesterday,' she told him.

'Yeah, I saw you too. I know what it looked like, but she was just a friend. It was just a goodbye kiss. Nothing much.'

Ashley was so relieved that he didn't have a girlfriend.

'Well. At least you told me,' she said.

'I wouldn't have kissed you if I already had a girlfriend. Would you like to go out on a date with me at the weekend? My treat!'

'I'd love to. As long as you're paying!'

They both started to laugh.

Paul took Ashley out on the date and paid. After that they went out nearly every weekend. They are still a couple and she loves her job.

WHY?

Megan Tyrrell

Stacy is a sixteen-year-old girl who lives in Kilbarrick. She lives with her adoptive mother and father. Her mum, Nicola, works in a bank in Coolock village and her father Brian is a carpenter. Stacy is an only child and she has a good relationship with her parents. She doesn't know that she is adopted.

****

One day her mum asked Stacy to clean out the attic. She agreed and went straight up to make a start. She was moving a few boxes around when she accidentally let one drop. Old letters spilled from the box onto the floor. As she was picking them up she found one that had her name on it. Stacy began to read the letter, and she couldn't believe what she was reading.

She looked at it again.

It said that she, Stacy, was adopted.

It had to be a joke.

She rushed downstairs to her mum to see who would have written something like this. When she showed her mum the letter, her mum just started to cry. Stacy then knew it must have been true; she was adopted.

She asked her mum why her birth mother gave her up.

'She just couldn't cope with a baby,' her mum replied.

Stacy then decided she wanted to find her birth mother and see why she gave her up. Stacy felt as if there was a part of her missing because she didn't know who her birth mum was. But the only thing that Nicola knew was her name: Leona Kerns.

Stacy began to look for Leona on the Internet, but after hours of searching she had no luck. So she decided she was going to go to the Rotunda Hospital to look for her birth records. Her mum and dad told her that it was a bad idea, that her real mum was not a nice person and she would only hurt her in the long run.

But Stacy would not give up. It was important to her.

Two days later Stacy was in the hospital. She was told to go to a woman called Alice Green who was in charge of the adoption unit. When she told Alice her name she realised that Alice knew her adoptive mum and dad. Because Stacy was sixteen, and old enough, Alice was able to give her the adoption records.

Stacy read through the file. She found out her mother was from Balbriggan and she was only sixteen when she'd had Stacy. She learned that when Leona was pregnant with Stacy she was highly addicted to drugs.

Stacy couldn't believe what she was reading. She had lots of questions for her birth mother but she didn't know if Leona could, or would, answer them.

The next day she decided she was going to go visit Leona. She needed to know what she was like before she could just forget about her. She didn't tell Nicola or Brian, her adoptive parents, where she was going. She didn't want to hurt their feelings after all they had done for her. Besides, she loved them.

The train journey from Kilbarrick out to Balbriggan took about twenty-five minutes, and all the way there Stacy felt sick with nerves.

Was she was making a big mistake?

She walked from the train station to a big estate with lots of children playing on a big green. She got to Leona's address – a large house with black and red bricks and big steps leading up to it.

She stood outside the house for a few minutes and she thought about going home, but then a tall, slim, blonde woman opened the door and asked her if she was OK.

Stacy asked what the woman's name was. She told Stacy her name was Sinéad.

Sinéad asked who Stacy was, and who she was looking for.

'Leona,' she said, trying not to show how nervous she was.

'Who are you?' the woman asked.

'Just a friend,' said Stacy.

'Leona's not in, but she'll be home soon. Do you want to come in and wait?' the woman asked.

Walking into the house, Stacy looked around to see if there were any signs of drug-taking in the house, but thankfully she didn't see anything odd. They sat in silence. Stacy was too afraid to reply when Sinéad made conversation – she didn't want to answer awkward questions about how she and Leona knew each other.

After about ten minutes, Stacy heard someone coming in the front door. She felt like getting up and running, but she knew there was no getting out of it now.

A pretty, tall, brown-haired woman walked into the kitchen where Stacy and Sinéad were sitting.

The woman looked at her and said: 'Do I know you?'

Stacy broke down in tears. She was crying so much she was not able to get the words out to tell her that she was her daughter. Leona did not know what was going on; she just kept asking Stacy if she was all right.

After a few minutes Stacy stopped crying and came out with it:

'I'm the child you gave away sixteen years ago.'

Leona started to cry. Stacy didn't know if they were tears of sadness or happiness. She just wanted her to stop crying so she could ask her questions.

'Would you like a cup of tea?' asked Leona through the tears. Stacy just wanted to get to the point, but a cup of tea would have to do for starters.

Stacy then asked the two things she wanted to know so badly.

'Why did you give me up at birth and where is my real father?'

Leona explained gently to her that the reason she did not keep her was because she was heavily addicted to heroin, and she would not have been able to cope with a baby. But Stacy would not settle for that excuse.

'Why could you not get help to get off drugs?' asked Stacy. But Leona didn't know how to answer that question. She told her that her real dad had passed away a few years ago from a drug overdose.

Leona then looked at her very seriously, cleared her throat and said: 'I have something else to tell you.' She told Stacy that she had two younger sisters, Milly who was three years old, and Shauna who was just gone fifteen.

Stacy couldn't believe it. She had never even thought about having any brothers or sisters. It turned out that a year after her mum gave her up for adoption she fell pregnant again with Shauna.

After a while they heard someone coming in the door. A tall, dark-haired girl walked into the kitchen. Stacy just stared at her.

Leona then said: 'Shauna, this is Stacy. She's my friend's daughter.'

Stacy was very hurt that Leona would not explain the situation.

Stacy stood up and mumbled, 'I have to go now,' and rushed out the door.

She made it as far as the end of the street. But then she walked back, scribbled her phone number onto a receipt she found in her pocket, and stuffed it through Leona's letterbox.

The next day was agony, but eventually Leona called.

'Hi Stacy, you left a bit quick yesterday. Would you like to come out this weekend?'

'Yes please,' said Stacy.

Later on she began to think how Nicola and Brian would feel about all of this. It took her a while to make up her mind, then she texted Leona: 'Sorry. I don't think it would be a good idea to meet up again.'

Stacy went into the kitchen where her mum and dad were sitting.

'I have something to tell you,' she said and saw that they both had a worried look on their faces. 'I went to meet Leona the other day.' She could see they were upset, but they both put a smile on for Stacy's sake.

Her mother asked her how she got on when she was out there.

'It was...not what I expected,' Stacy replied. She showed her parents the message she had sent to Leona.

'Why don't you want to go?' asked her mum.

'They're not my family. I have all the people I need here.'

Nicola and Brian smiled at her. Then they hugged each other.

A year on, Stacy has had no contact with Leona, and she is happy with who she is. She loves her parents: the only ones she knows. All the rest is history.

Notes on the Authors

Emma Browne is sixteen years old and goes to secondary school. She is in Transition Year. When she first attended the Fighting Words programme, she was excited to meet the famous authors and to get started on writing her story. On the first day she didn't really like it. She was expecting it to be more fun, but it was hard work. She didn't attend the programme for two weeks after the first week because she didn't like it. But her year head convinced her to go back to finish her story. She started to get the hang of the programme and got stuck into her story. She loves the story that she came up with and wants to thank everyone who helped her in the programme and her year head.

Klaudia Bucka is a sixteen-year-old student in Coláiste Dhúlaigh. She was born in Krakow, Poland, but in 2007 she moved to Ireland. Her best friends are Paula, Arek and Oskar. She loves photography, reading books and travel. She speaks Polish and English, and is also starting to learn French. Klaudia says, '*Mam nadzieje, ie polubicie moja historie* – I hope you will like my story.'

Megan Burke is in Transition Year in Coláiste Dhúlaigh. She lives in Kilmore. She loves going out with her friends and having a laugh. She likes going out on the weekends and doing something fun. She doesn't really like school, as she hates getting up in the morning. But she wants to be a solicitor, so she has to go to school.

Hughie Collins lives with his mother in Coolock. He goes to Coláiste Dhúlaigh and is in the class of McAleese. He's sixteen years old. He wants to go to college. He doesn't know what he wants to study yet. He loves football and music when he's outside of school. His favourite subjects are PE and History. He liked writing this story. He found it very interesting. It is his first time writing a proper story.

Gary Duffy is in Fourth Year at Coláiste Dhúlaigh. He is sixteen and likes music and games. He lives with his two sisters, three brothers and his mother.

Eve Gibney is a sixteen-year-old student. She's from Coolock. She lives with her ma, da and baby sister and her three fish Peppa, George and Linkin. She enjoys spending her time hanging around with her friends. She's an aspiring hairdresser and make-up artist. She greatly appreciated this opportunity to write a short story.

Sarah Gorry is fifteen years old and she is in Transition Year in Coláiste Dhúlaigh. She likes hanging around with her friends and spends most of her time in the skate park in Blanchardstown. She describes herself as a quiet and private person. She loves writing in her spare time and thinks this was a great project to be involved with.

Shannon Granger lives in Coolock. She is in Transition Year. She finds it very boring, but they go on trips and it's good fun. She loves going to school to see her friends and to have a laugh. She loves going out at the weekends with her friends. When she is older she wants to be a fashion designer as she likes fashion a lot.

Danielle Hand is a sixteen-year-old student in Coláiste Dhúlaigh. She is in Transition Year. She was born on 15 January 1995 in Rotunda Hospital, Dublin. She is living in Coolock, and has been for the past twelve years. She loves writing and in her spare time she plays with her dog Snowy or just sits in her bedroom singing along with the music. She also loves kids. She is a person who loves to be around funny people. Danielle also loves to be out with her friends having a good time.

Eoghan Higgins is sixteen years old. This is his first year in Coláiste Dhúlaigh and it has been good fun. He had a mentor called Joan and she helped him. He found writing the story good. He found it a great opportunity to become a young published author. The volunteers in Fighting Words said he wrote like a journalist. He loves football and that is what his story is about. He enjoys socialising with his friends and generally having a good time. He thinks he would like to go to college to do a business course.

Alan Keegan is sixteen and lives in Coolock with his mam and his sister. He likes football and playing sports and going out with his friends. He thought writing the book was fun. He is looking forward to seeing the book published, so he can show it to his friends and family. He would like to thank the mentor who helped him write the story. He goes to Coláiste Dhúlaigh and it is a good school because the students are awesome and they have a laugh and they get on well with the teachers. He is currently in Transition Year and will be going into Fifth Year next year.

Damien McKevitt is fifteen years old. He is in Transition Year in Coláiste Dhúlaigh, Coolock. His interests include watching sports and playing snooker. He thinks he would like go to college when he leaves school, but he doesn't know what he'd like to study yet. Damien has two more years to decide. He lives in Coolock with his dad and his two brothers.

Tomás Nguyen is sixteen years old. He really enjoyed writing this story. He thought it was the best thing in Transition Year. When he is not in school, Tomás enjoys going out with his friends. He wants to be a mechanic when he leaves school.

Karen Nolan is sixteen years old and a Transition Year student at Coláiste Dhúlaigh. She lives in Coolock. Her interests are going out with her friends and going shopping. She found writing the story interesting. She learned a lot about how to write a story and met new people and they helped her to write her story. She wants to be a hairdresser when she leaves school.

Megan Tyrrell is in Transition Year. She doesn't really like school, she thinks it's a bit boring, but she likes when they go out on trips and have other things to do. She loves going out with friends, having a laugh and going on walks to keep fit. She is really into fashion and loves going shopping. Megan wants to be a solicitor so she's going to have to stay in school and study very hard.